Camille's Second Chance
Clearwater Daddies
Book 2
Alyssa Bailey

ALYSSA BAILEY

Camille's Second Chance

Alyssa Bailey ©2023 All rights reserved.

Alyssa Bailey

Camille's Second Chance

Paperback ISBN:

Description of Camille's Second Chance

"We're going to the ranch. *This Daddy is taking care of all his little ones.*"

Before she was twenty-one, Camille Hendrix had been lied to, cheated on, assaulted twice, forced into a loveless marriage, divorced, and left to fend for herself with one baby and another on the way. She had also been loved by a man she left without a word of explanation and missed every day of her life. Now, with a nursing degree and two preschoolers she was determined to return to her hometown and make a life, if possible, with the only man she ever loved. But was it too much to ask? Someone in town thought so.

Sawyer Knight was the most sought-after playboy in three counties and probably more. Everyone knew the woman he loved had suddenly left town without a word. Since then, Sawyer could be seen most weekends at the Whet Whistle, kicking up dust, getting toasted, and going home with a different woman. No woman was permanent in his life and Sawyer made that known loud and clear, until Cami came back to town. She was divorced, a mother, and life weary but when he laid eyes on her in his brother's house, she was still the most beautiful, feisty woman he'd ever seen. Maybe more than ever because her strength of character shone through the battle scars

1

and his heart immediately yearned for her. If he claimed her this time, he wouldn't let her go without a fight. It seemed the first opponent had already entered the ring.

Love the inside scoop? Sign up for my Newsletter with special offers and bonus content.

https://www.alyssabaileyromance.com

Chapter 1

Camille audibly sighed as she pulled into her childhood home. She was glad to have arrived, but apprehensive about her choice of destinations. Cami focused her weary eyes on the house she grew up in. The half-light gave it a sinister shadow. She was positive she imagined the darkness. When did it take on the look of sadness? Coming back was a hard decision made harder as she stared at the home she grew up in.

For the thousandth time since they drove onto the Alaska Marine Highway's Ferry, MV Tongass Rain, she wondered if she had made the right decision. After all, she had secrets, sorrow and two children she adored returning to a community with a long memory and a short attention span.

The last six years hadn't been easy, but she had survived, thrived even. Much to the incredulity of her parents. I lost Camille after ending a horrible but blessedly short marriage forced on her by her parents. She'd hated herself and her parents for much longer than the ten months she was married. But that was all water under the bridge.

The house and yard looked exactly the same as it did when she left almost six years ago. Lilies and various color-coordinated flowerbeds were displaying the same reds, blues, oranges and yellows they always had. Camille saw herself as clearly today as that fateful day her world came crumbling down around her.

She'd stood crying, begging her parents, Ronnie and Carla Hendrix, on that very doorstep in front of her now. She pleaded with them to reconsider, let her stay, and figure something out, but it hadn't happened that way. Camille told her mother the man they wanted her to marry forced her, but it made no difference. Carla Hendrix never actually said she didn't believe her, but she left her distraught daughter with no misunderstanding about the expectations.

Her counselor later told her they had, by their actions, raped her again. Camille thought that was a harsher verdict than she could subscribe to because she played a part in the whole fiasco. She'd been too weak to stand up against them. She spent years believing they were to blame for her loss of the only man she'd ever loved. Later, she'd had to admit she'd left him too easily, thinking he wouldn't want her. She had called Sawyer that fateful morning, but he was working on the ranch and he didn't pick up.

Her sole message, "I love you, Sawyer. I don't know if I can ever survive without you. There isn't anything I can do to stop what is happening. I'm sorry for everything."

She didn't know if he'd called her back. Her parents had kept her phone. She never had another until the day Aiden had left her for another woman. On that day, she took back control of her life. She called a domestic assault hotline from the doctor's office and was offered a phone. Once Aiden had found out about Eli's parentage, was when she took the bigger lifeline, freedom.

She was placed into protective housing, given legal advice, offered a pro-bono attorney and finally got an emergency phone line. She had a phone but no access to long distance and no disposable funds to purchase a calling card. It was too late to mend fences by the time she did. She had no choice but to look forward.

She'd regretted too many things in her life. This was a new beginning. No more regrets. Aiden Blevins wanted the girl he thought was related to the big-time criminal lawyer and if she was pregnant, it was an inconvenience but not the end of the world. When he found out she not only wasn't carrying his child but also was not related to the attorney who had her last name, he wanted out, and fast. The mistake had been his assumptions because she was met in that attorney's home. She was a tutor to the man's child, not his relative regardless of the same odd last name.

Aiden took a job in Alaska, dragging her along with him, even though she had begged to stay nearer to home. Later she found out it was because of how easily he could get divorced. It was probably the fastest divorce known to modern man and then he sent her packing. As an attorney, it had been child's play for him.

Cami had learned she had no one to rely on but herself. One of her greatest regrets was she'd never contacted Sawyer. She'd hurt him too badly to expect any kind of help from him. She didn't deserve it, anyway, no matter how much she still carried a torch for him.

Cami found a knowledgeable social worker who helped her qualify for a grant to get her certified nurse's assistant license before Eli was born, helped her with housing after the divorce, and taught her general tricks to living on her own with a child. Later she had gotten her nursing degree and license and she began to make enough money to feel like she could breathe.

She helped her change her name to Hendrix Knight. Not a hyphen, but two separate names. See, Cami had one dream she refused to give up on, even though it was out of reach.

Her parents didn't know about the degree, the circumstances of her second child, Piccadilly or anything else. They had only learned of her divorce when she called last month. Camille had no intention of sharing much of her personal history since they'd forced her out. She was still bitter in some ways, and there was no reason to make her parents' life any easier.

She had a lead on several rentals owned by Piper Gentry that she could afford. Piper said at least one of them would be perfect. She'd hold them for her until she arrived. Piper confided that she was now a Knight and they had just announced they were pregnant. Piper's family owned the Gentry place next to Clear Knight Ranch, Sawyer's family's place. She was happy for Piper, but it put a spotlight on the fact that Cami had allowed others to force her to walk away from that future that had been planned for herself.

She shook her head and looked back at the loves of her life. Eli, named after his father, lay on the back seat, his hand curled in sleep around his sister, Lily. Her chest tightened at the rush of love she felt looking at her children. She'd do anything for them, starting with introducing them to their grandparents and Eli to his father.

Well, no reason to delay the inevitable any longer. Her parents were standing at the door of the house now, presumably waiting to meet their grandchildren. They'd been stunned to hear from her a month ago. Her mother cried. It cracked a small bit of Cami's hardened heart. Only a little. Forgiveness was a long way off.

The interior light came on and a rush of humid heat overwhelmed her for a moment. Eli, so much like his father, pulled his sister in close and tried to open his intelligent light blue eyes despite his deep state of sleep. They often sparkled like his father's did once upon a time.

"Are we at my daddy's house?" he asked in a sleep roughened little voice.

Her heart hitched. She moved the wild honey blonde curl from his face, just as she had done with Sawyer so many times before.

"Sorry, little man, but we are at Grandma and Grandpa's house. Do you want to meet them? I'll take care of Miss Lily."

"Okay, Mama. But is my daddy here?"

"No, love. We'll see him soon. I promise." *If he will see you after I tell him I have kept you from him for five years, that is.* But something deep inside told her Sawyer Knight would accept his son unconditionally. She and his sister was another story. *One thing at a time, girl.*

Scooping her small daughter up from the safety chair after Eli had scrambled out, Cami gazed down at her. Lily looked like her mother, sharing her brown eyes but Lily's hair was a dark blonde, a combination of Cami's darker brown and Aiden's light blonde.

Time to enter the lions' den. *Hope they've had dinner.*

When had her four-year-old gotten so heavy Cami wondered as she followed Elijah's solemn walk. She grabbed her purse and slung it over her shoulder while juggling Eli's still groggy sister to meet Ronnie and Carla Hendrix, their grand-parents.

"Hi Mom, Dad. We made it," said Camille with as much false cheerfulness as she could muster.

Her mother looked sad for a moment and even glanced at the car, looking for Aiden, Cami imagined. "Mom, we're divorced." She almost added *for five years* but decided she'd not make things worse than they were. "But I did bring your grand-children to meet you."

"Grandchildren?" she asked as though she had forgotten about Lily. "Oh, yes, and we have been waiting a long time to meet them."

The reproach was loud and clear to which, mentally, Cami replied, *"We didn't live in another country. You could have visited anytime you'd cared to come."* Verbally, she said, "They've been curious as well."

Camille knew her children were tired and needed a bed. They were what was important. If Piper Gentry could get one apartment ready quickly, she'd definitely snag one and move in quickly. It was never going to be a good relationship with her parents. Too much of life had passed.

"We're tired and hot, Mom. Do you think we could come in?"

Stunned for a moment, as though she had forgotten they were on the front porch in the twilight of the evening, Carla didn't move. Ronnie pushed his wife out of the way to allow their visitors inside. Lily had gone back to sleep, and Ronnie put his hands out to take her. Cami hesitated, but relinquished her daughter.

"I believe your mother has the children in your old room. You can have the bedroom next door.

"Dad, we'll sleep together, so whichever room has the bigger bed would be more comfortable for us. I don't want the children waking in a strange place without me close at hand."

Ronnie looked at Carla as though asking if they could change her plan. Nothing had changed in the pecking order around here, then. "Well, if that's going to upset you, I can easily go to a hotel. However, since we plan to stay only a night or two, I thought you would like to get to know them."

"Ronnie, put her in the room with Camille." He left to do his wife's bidding. It was clear that he was not following Cami's request, but his wife's.

"Lily. Her name is Lily or Piccadilly, if you like."

Carla opened her mouth and Cami waited for her mother to say something and then, miracle of all miracles, she didn't. Instead, she looked down into the serious face, observing her intently.

"And you, my boy, must be Aiden."

"Eli," said both mother and son in unison.

Cami grabbed Eli's hand and walked him to the living room, where she put on the light and sat down, pulling him to sit next to her. She knew it was as much for her own nerves as any awkwardness or worry her son might have. He loved to laugh, but if it was important, he was all business. She could see Sawyer in the way he placed his hand, not in hers but over the top, in a move of protection. She turned hers over to clasp his in a show of support and comfort.

"Eli? You said he was named after his father."

"He is."

"Yes, my first name is my daddy's middle name."

"Ah." Carla nodded as though that answered her query, but it didn't, not really. Cami was not enlightening her.

Time to take control of the conversation so her mother didn't think she'd kowtow to her as she had in the years of her childhood. "Mom, I have appointments tomorrow morning and the children should get some sleep before we head out. I anticipate staying a couple of days if that won't put you out."

"I planned on you staying here for a while. I mean, you have no husband to help you."

"Thank you, but no. I assure you I have done quite well without the man you forced... without Aiden."

Eli looked at his mother and asked quietly, "Mama, are we going to see my daddy soon?"

"Yes, sweetheart, tomorrow or the next day, I imagine. I'll call him tomorrow."

Eli tried to suppress a yawn while he nodded in understanding.

"Oh, so Aiden is coming. Well, that's a relief. Raising children away from their father isn't a good idea."

"Okay, we are off to bed. Say good night to your grandmother, Eli."

"Good night, grandmother."

As they passed Ronnie on their way up to the bedroom, Eli reached out his hand to shake the older gentleman's. A wide grin spread across Ronnie's face, then he solemnly shook his grandson's hand.

"Good night, Dad," said Camille.

"Night you two. See you in the morning."

Sleep was elusive for Cami, but thankfully not for her children. As she lay, trying not to toss and turn, she thought of the things she needed to get done before the school year started. Her job began the day before the pupils so she could get the nurse's station set up, but there was final hire paperwork she needed to complete. She had hoped that she could ask her mother to watch the children while she finished the setting up of their new life, but she couldn't risk it at this stage. Not until she had spoken to Sawyer.

Sawyer. How was she going to tell him? She knew she had to, but no matter how many times she had the whole scenario set up in her head, it never sounded good enough. It wasn't as though she was looking for a romantic relationship with him. Cami shook her head mentally at herself. No more lies, not to herself or to Sawyer.

She still dreamed of the relationship she had with him before she'd left. She was under no illusions that a relationship would be possible now, but she wanted him to love his son. Eventually, she fell into an exhausted sleep, in bed with two little blonde headed heaters.

The quiet chatter woke Camille up with a start. Disoriented, she called out to the children.

"Mama, Mama, we are in someone's bedroom," declared Lily in worried hushed tones as though they had made some grave error.

"It's okay Lily Bug, we are in Mama's kid home, remember?" said Eli in typical big brother fashion.

"Childhood home, dear." Camille didn't dare crack a smile, for Eli wouldn't have appreciated that. She needed a shower and coffee. "I bet you are ready for your breakfast."

"Does your child's home have cereal?"

"I imagine we can find some. Let's go see what there is to eat, shall we?"

Both children leapt from the bed, jumping up and down but not opening the door. The motels they had stayed at on the way to Texas weren't the best, but Camille couldn't imagine paying much for a night of sleep. For protection, she had drilled into the children they were never to open a door in a place they didn't know. The lesson had taken well, and she was proud of them.

"Thank you for waiting until I opened the door. Now let's go find breakfast."

As they walked down the stairs, everything looked different in the daylight and yet, all was familiar. She walked into the kitchen and settled the children at the table before reaching to open the cupboard that historically had held cereal. Bran flakes. No children lived in the house now and the cereal selection announced that fact.

"No cereal. Let's see what else they have, shall we?" Doing a bit more rummaging, she found toaster waffles, microwave sausage and orange juice. It would have to do.

Just as she was finishing things up, her mother appeared. "Oh, you aren't giving them that for breakfast, are you? Your father buys that when he wants something fast. It's not a proper breakfast."

"They would have done fine with cereal, but bran flakes aren't their favorite. I'll grab a box when we do errands."

"You can't be serious."

"Mom, you fed us cereal all the time as kids." To which Carla said nothing. "I'm grabbing a cup of coffee and going to take a quick shower. The kids will be fine. Send them up when they are done so they can dress. I'm on a schedule today."

"Of course, but what about Aiden?"

Camille pointedly glanced at her children before walking to the far end of the kitchen. Her mother followed. Camille spoke in a low voice.

"What about him?"

"I thought he was coming."

"Really? Why would you think that? We aren't married. And for your information, we haven't been for five years. We technically lived together for ten months. We were divorced within one year. I didn't initiate it, Aiden did, but I was relieved. It probably saved my life. He had a new lady friend before the papers were filed. They have been married for three years. I think. The children have heard of him, but except for Eli as a newborn, the children have never seen him."

"But Eli said he was going to see his father."

"He is." Camille turned away, leaving her mother and her coffee in the kitchen. Damn, she needed that coffee.

Shower done, children dressed, she left to complete her employment paperwork. She just needed a photo ID, to sign a few things, and get a tour of the school. Her medical pre-screenings were all done at the hospital before she left. All the schools were on the same campus but in separate buildings. Her office was centrally located between the elementary and junior high schools, where she imagined she'd be most needed. During the tour, her personnel guide pointed out the kindergarten and preschool rooms for Lily and Elijah.

The attentive young man, Karl, who showed her the school, offered his assistance at any time. He was attractive enough, but she had never had eyes for anyone but Sawyer. And after her fiasco of a forced marriage, it was survival. Then the children came, and they'd been her only focus.

Karl appeared to be a little older than she was and was full of helpful information. She'd make sure to take him up on his offer of help if needed. He gave her the keys to her office and finished the tour by showing her a few more essential places, like the teachers' lounge and the supply closet. They were done by noon.

Cami needed to feed the children before they looked at the duplex. They'd done well for their ages, but she needed space for them to run and food to keep them happy this afternoon. She walked over to the café next to Gentry World Investments, GWI, on the logo.

This used to be a favorite hangout as a teen, and she liked that it was still open. Settling the children in the booth with an enormous window to the street, Cami was helping her offspring decide just how hungry they were when she saw Piper, who had her picture on her website, step out of the passenger side of a pickup. She was helped down by the man she had hoped not to run into until she had decided how to speak to him.

She watched in horror as Sawyer handed Piper out of the truck, said a few words, laid his hand on her almost flat tummy, and dropped a kiss on her cheek before climbing back into the driver's seat, pulling away from the curb. Cami's worst nightmare had come to roost. Sawyer was married and evidently, to Piper Gentry.

Chapter 2

Piper had said she was a Knight now, and that they had just announced their first child was on the way. The way Sawyer was so sweet to her, he must be the Knight brother Piper had married. Not Jackson, as she had first thought. They had been an item before going to college. Jackson must have worked through the loss to his brother, or had he?

What was she going to do now? Piper was in the position Cami had once expected herself to be in. Could she rent from her? Would she be able to deal with Sawyer in love with another woman? Having children with her? And what about her Eli? Would Sawyer reject him in the face of his and Piper's child? No, she would never allow Eli to be hurt.

The children had a wonderful time at lunch while their mama was on the verge of tears the whole meal. The lovely man, Karl, stepped in to grab a lunch he obviously had pre-ordered and she smiled at him. He grinned back and tipped his cowboy hat in greeting. Cami thought he'd come over to the table, but seemed to change his mind. It felt good for someone to offer her a genuine smile, instead of the curious pasted-on ones she had encountered most of the day. Small towns and their long memories, especially when they didn't have the truth of their remembered rumors.

Cami settled on grilled cheese for the kids, and the waitress brought their annual Rodeo coloring contest pages and crayons for the kids to create their masterpieces. Lily, a free spirit, was wildly creative in her color choices. While Eli laughed at Lily's adventuresome kaleidoscope, he carefully colored in the lines. Entries submitted with the waitress, lunches eaten, and bathroom break complete, Cami led the much calmer children next door.

A young lady looked up as the little group entered GWI and greeted them with an attempt at a smile. "Good afternoon. Can I help you?"

The cool air was welcomed after even the few moments spent in the sweltering hot air. The children didn't seem to notice the heat as much as she did. Nearly six years in Alaska put her at a disadvantage in the August heat of Texas. She needed to carry more water in the car and get the kids hats, lotion and sunshades.

They'd like that.

"Yes, I'm here to see Piper. I'm Camille—"

"Hendrix, yes, I have you right here." Glad that Piper had supplied the name she remembered Cami with, she didn't have to disclose her full name publicly. Not yet anyway.

"Camille, how are you?" Piper came out and hugged Cami like they were long-lost friends. Piper had been three grades ahead of her in Sawyer's class, so it surprised her the executive remembered her at all. Stepping back, Piper looked at the two children standing close to their mama. "Oh, they are beautiful."

"I think so." Camille smiled in the cheerful woman's company. How could she resist? Especially when Piper was saying sweet things about her children?

"What are your names?"

Lily hid behind Cami's leg, but Eli spoke up. "That's Lily. She's four and kinda shy. I'm Elijah and I'm five. I have my daddy's name."

"Oh, well, they are both lovely names." Piper looked at Lily and then back at Cami. "She looks so much like you. And Elijah must look like his daddy."

"Yes, I do. I have my daddy's looks and his name. Except my first name is his second name, so we don't get confused."

"Okay, Eli, that's enough. Poor Mrs. Knight has work to do." Cami looked over at Piper with as bland a look as she could create. She hoped it worked.

"Knight? That's our name. Well, Hendrix Knight but—"

"Eli," said Cami firmly. "We are bothering Miss Piper. Don't you want to get the keys and look at our new place?"

Piper nodded. "Right. Linda, take the children into the conference room and get them going on some entertainment or turn on the cable. Cami and I have some catching up to do."

Camille almost bolted,, but she'd have to deal with Sawyer's wife at some point. Since she wanted to rent from her, it might as well be now. Goodbye rental. Hello classifieds. Piper led Cami into the office and closed the door.

"Have a seat." Piper stared at the forms on her desk for a moment before looking into Camille's eyes. "I'm not one to beat around the bush."

"I figured." Cami sighed. "What do you want to know?"

"Um, everything? But let's start with the disclosure. Who is Eli's father?"

Camille considered for a brief second to lie, but the look on Piper's face told her it wouldn't work for long, if at all. "Sawyer."

"I take it he doesn't know."

Not the reaction she expected. "Of course not. I didn't know until I was halfway through my pregnancy. I was too far along for him to be Aiden's baby."

"Aiden. I assume that is your husband?"

"Ex."

"Okay, but why not his?"

Cami didn't know how much to tell and decided it would get easier with the first telling, so she let all the information tumble out. The part about Aiden thinking she was related to the important attorney with the same name. Forcing himself on her to convince her parents they needed to marry. Her frightening discovery several weeks later, and how she was too naïve to realize she could have already been pregnant since she and Sawyer had made love recently.

Cami explained her parents forcing her out or to marry Aiden and since she didn't want to tell Sawyer she was pregnant with another man's child, she left with the man her parents were demanding she marry. Trouble was, on the wedding night in Vegas, when he found out she wasn't related to the attorney. She was only his son's tutor. Aiden had gone ballistic.

"He hit me once that night, but never again. Aiden was too smart for that. He had forced himself on me previously." Cami took a deep breath and let it out before shaking her head. "No, he raped me. But now that he knew I was pregnant, he didn't want me to press criminal charges. He knew better than I did what I could have done to his career, his future freedom, and more. Needless to say, our marriage was over that night. If it ever had a chance, that is."

"Oh, Cami, why didn't you come home? Jackson says Sawyer got lost after you left. He figures Sawyer never quite recovered."

"Me either. I missed him so much. I mean..." Piper pushed the tissue box in her direction. "We both still thought Eli was Aiden's at that point. By the time I figured it out, Aiden had another girlfriend and rarely came home for long, thankfully. Anyway, when Eli was born, I already knew he was Sawyer's. Two months early. Anyway, without my permission or knowledge, he had a DNA test done and verified Eli wasn't his."

"Oh, honey, I'm so sorry. What happened next?" Piper gave her a bottle of water.

"As you can imagine, it was the out he was looking for. He came home drunk the night he got the results back." Cami took a drink of the water, working hard to control the tremor in her voice. "Eli was about three months and he forced himself on me. He was rough, out of control, and I screamed." Cami shrugged. "We lived in a little detached house so no one could hear me."

She drew her legs up in the wide chair, planting her feet on the seat and her arms around her knees. "Anyway, as my luck would have it, he raped me again that night. The only two times we had sex and they were rapes. He was so much stronger than I was. By then I had an emergency phone. I turned it on to record when he came toward me. He stumbled and I hit the record app fast. I said all the right things to make it stick. See, I had learned from my attorney husband and my recent counseling that it was important to have a plan."

Cami shrugged and wiped the tears from her cheek. "He was accommodating in his drunken state, to admit to raping me the first time, and then went on to do it again."

"I'm so sorry. I guess that is where Lily came from?"

"You guessed right. I never had sex with him again. Twice. That was it. The first time ruined my life, the second time gave me it back. He doesn't even know she exists."

"Did your parents not come to your aid?"

"I never told them."

"Oh, but..." she stopped when she saw Cami shake her head. Piper continued softly. "And Sawyer?"

"I don't know. I didn't think he'd believe me about Eli. And Lily? Who would want another man's child?"

"Sawyer would. Besides, he will guess about Eli the first time he sees him. That boy looks just like him when he was a kid."

Cami straightened up in her seat again, sniffing back the last of her tears. "Not after I left without speaking to him directly. I didn't have a phone afterward. Then I had so much I was worried about. I got a divorce with sole custody and Aiden relinquished rights based on DNA and gave me spousal support for my promise not to release the recording. He'd have lost his job and likely gone to jail. Probably been disbarred. With lots of help, I had Lily, earned a degree and came back here."

"You have to tell him."

"I will. Eli should know his dad. I had no idea how much trouble it would cause with me coming back. I'm sorry, Piper. Really, I don't want to cause a strain on your marriage."

"My marriage?" She shook her head. "Other than my husband wanting to draw and quarter your ex, it won't bother my marriage."

"But it could put a strain on it and with you having a little one on the way. I just don't want Elijah hurt."

Piper considered Cami for a moment and then scrunched up her face before speaking again. "I'm missing something here."

"The kids and I had lunch at the café today. We saw you in the window."

Piper's face cleared and she grinned. Actually grinned. "You saw me get out of Sawyer's truck."

Camille nodded. "He really loves you." Her voice held pain and envy.

"Well I hope so, since I'm carrying around his first niece or nephew."

Now it was Cami's turn to scrunch her face. "Not his child?"

Piper laughed. "The brothers are close, I grant you that, but I don't think Jackson would want to share his wife and I damn sure don't want his brothers."

Cami didn't even know how tense she was until she heard Piper laugh. He wasn't married to Piper. What a relief!

"And before you ask, he hasn't had a steady girlfriend since you left, I'm told. No wife, no ex, no fiancée, nothing. I don't know how he was with you in your relationship, but that man is likely to spank you raw when he finds out you could have come to him all those years ago. That he could have been there for his son's babyhood and been a father to Lily."

"Is it too late? Am I too late?"

Piper sobered. "Honestly, I don't know. But you have to tell him so he can be there for Eli. You don't have a choice."

"That's why I came back."

"And to see if Sawyer would give you another chance?"

"Yes."

Linda knocked on the door and called in with a rather desperate voice. "The natives are getting restless out here."

"Coming right out!"

"Okay, you get the keys from Linda and pick your duplex. I'll get a contract together. You gave Eli the last name of Knight."

"Well, I changed our names back to my maiden name in the divorce and then added Knight so we would have the same last name, but he'd have his father's name. When Lily was born, I gave her my name, Hendrix Knight. I figured, if Sawyer was upset about it, Lily and I can use my maiden name in daily usage."

"Okay, go pick out your duplex."

It had been a long day and Cami was beat, but she'd gotten so much done, she was proud of herself. After deciding on which home would work best for them, she took the kids to an open field and let them run around burning off energy. Even though she had allowed them to race through the duplex, they needed more. It wasn't until they were tired and ready to go home, did she think about snakes and the like. She hadn't worried about reptiles in Alaska, but they were in Texas now.

At the table that evening, Carla Hendrix had been subdued and Ronnie had tried to keep up a conversation with the children, but it seemed as though they were all too preoccupied or too tired to do more than eat.

"Thank you for dinner. I'll put the kids to bed and then come out to clean up."

"I can handle that. You take care of the children."

"I can do it when I'm finished."

The mulish expression her mother often wore when she faced any opposition appeared, effectively ending the conversation. "Thanks, Mom. Then if you two don't mind, I'm bushed. I think we might move into the duplex tomorrow. I'll let you know." Carla's only reply was a nod.

The children were overtired and fussy. It had been a long month and the last two weeks had been brutal for all of them. She needed to get them back into their own place. Tomorrow, things would begin to look up. And today had yielded some good results, including finding out no woman could claim Sawyer Knight.

Chapter 3

Rumor had it she was back. His Cami was back and with two little ones. She had left town and if you put any stock in the chatter, she had shown up yesterday, tired, with a loaded car, Alaska plates and children. What the hell had happened to her? Sawyer wasn't sure he wanted to see her and was damned sure he couldn't keep away.

Children. Fuck they should have been his children. Hell, he'd turned down a good time lay last night, feeling as though he were cheating on Cami. On what they had and she had two children. What was wrong with him? But the reality was, that wasn't anything new. Even when he had tried to start over with another woman, he felt he was cheating. Evidently, she hadn't felt the same way. His gut seized with guilt, anger and longing for his girl. And now she was back.

The feed store owner's wife was speaking to another rancher's wife. "Things don't look like they have changed for that Camille Hendrix or whatever her name is now. That girl isn't right in the head if you ask me. Flighty. She was crying like crazy the night before she left, told my daughter there wasn't anything anyone could do for her. She had to leave town. Next morning, she was gone."

The woman shook her head as she rang up the sales tags from the feedbags Sawyer had loaded in the back of his pickup.

The owner continued her gossip. "My Bonnie said it was like the hounds of Hell were after her. Now she's back with no husband and two kids. Guess we know why she had to leave. One looks a boy about five, I heard. The other, a girl, is younger. Heard she went to her mom's house. Got a job as the school district nurse. Not sure we want to have that sort as our children's nurse."

"And just what sort of girl is that? A mother? A hometown girl?" asked a now pissed off Sawyer.

"A girl, who would leave at the drop of any trouble, with loose morals. I heard it told she left you, Sawyer Knight."

"How far is the nearest feed store, I wonder? It might be worth going to another place that is less judgmental of others' misfortunes." He tipped his hat and walked away.

Before he left the store, he heard the other rancher's wife. "You know he and Camille were an item for as long as I can remember. And he is part of the two biggest ranch operations for counties. You might not want to make him angry."

Sawyer smiled through his frustration. It was a lot of responsibility on most days, but sometimes it was good to be a Knight.

Riding back to the ranch, Sawyer thought about what the woman had said and thought back to that terrible day he found out Camille was gone. It gutted him. Now she was back. He wanted to see her but even if she wanted nothing to do with him, he'd allow no one to talk bad about his girl. She'd been his since the first time he laid eyes on her on a trail ride with several other young girls at a birthday party. She was in the sixth grade, looking and acting older. He was in the ninth grade. He found out her name and never looked back.

He'd kept his hands off her until she was in ninth grade, but he spent as much time as he could with her until then. He loved her. There was no doubt about his feelings, and he'd thought she felt the same way about him until that day. Even then, he thought something was off, odd, wrong. He always thought her parents had something to do with it even though they denied it.

They had told him she didn't want anything to do with him anymore and he knew that wasn't true. She had always been a pleaser, choosing to avoid conflict at all costs and her parents had never wanted her to spend time at the ranch or with him. Especially with him. He was destined to be a rancher and her mother, especially, saw no future in it. He had to laugh. He made more money than most physicians in a year.

Clear Knight Ranch had done some rearranging over the last couple of years and since his brother Jackson had married Piper, Gentry Ranch joined Clear Knight under a new corporate umbrella, Clearwater Corporation. They'd worked hard to make things work better. Piper bought out her siblings on the Gentry place and changed the name to Clearwater Ranch. She had wanted to consolidate both places, but the Knight men decided they wanted to keep the ranches separate businesses, so they formed a corporation.

Jackson still worked his breeding program but had created a gate between Clear Knight and Clearwater so he could work both areas. He had moved over the non-technical parts of breeding and some of his training stock, onto a piece of land that butted up to the Knight land and hired Jason Kirkland for Clearwater's manager.

Now, Walker and Sawyer ran Clear Knight Ranch themselves with the three brothers coming together on decisions bigger than day-to-day operations. They had settled into a nice routine. Josie, Walker's girlfriend, spent a little more time with Walker at the ranch once again since the big blowup over the Piper Incident, as they called it. Walker was on cloud nine when Josie began dating him again, even if he was tiptoeing on that cloud, so he didn't upset the balance.

Sawyer had ended the last of many wounded half-hearted relationships a few months ago and it hurt when everyone around him was content. He was happy for them, but his own future love life looked no better than his past.

He didn't think his luck would end as well as Jackson's had with Piper, who had come back after ten years of avoiding his brother. They'd gotten married and the couple had just announced their first child to arrive in seven months. Piper had added pregnancy to her hectic life and Jackson, with calm determination, took off other responsibilities while she complained.

Ultimately, she agreed with some extra persuasion from Daddy Jackson. That was how their relationship worked. It was how his and Cami's had worked until she all but disappeared with nothing but a cryptic message on his machine. That along with what he heard today made the mystery even more confusing.

It wasn't the kids so much, although he wanted them, it was the companionship he missed. He and Camille had that special something, even though he was three years older than she was, her maturity was impressive. She didn't balk at staying and running the ranch with him and the others. He'd made plans to build their place on his piece of the ranch before she had graduated. After graduation, they both worked hard to earn enough money to make their dream a reality.

Then, out of the blue, she was unavailable and in less than a week, she had left him a tearful message. He had memorized it. "I love you, Sawyer. I don't know if I can ever survive without you. There isn't anything I can do. I'm sorry for everything." He must've replayed that message daily for nearly a year.

That had been the very last time he'd heard from her. He'd called her phone, but it went to voice mail the first week before it was disconnected. He'd gone to her parents' home and was told she had simply left with someone named Aiden Blevins, an attorney. No, they had no idea where she was. They didn't expect her back and he should get on with his life. He had held his bleeding heart for over a year and then tucked it away. His reputation had changed soon afterwards from the man who lost at love to the man who was looking for a good time without commitments. There were plenty of takers hoping to change his mind. He hadn't.

Now he was tired of it all. He'd rodeoed for a few years but hated the time away from the ranch. Besides, he had rodeoed to get money to start their lives. It hadn't happened. He was a rancher. It was in his blood. He'd already had to purge one thing he thought vital from his life, he wouldn't suffer another loss. He quit the rodeo and came back to the ranch full time. Along with his brothers, he'd poured his heart and soul into making it what it was today.

Jackson bred cattle; Sawyer bred horses. Walker, the eldest, was the best ranch businessman they knew. He ran the entire operation from his desk and atop a horse. Walker and Piper worked well when implementing their coordinated business plans, but Jackson and Sawyer worked those plans to perfection. The ranches were thriving. They had taken on extra hands. One of the best investments they'd made.

Walker had decided to go to Austin for the weekend as he often did these days, leaving Friday night. Sawyer went over to eat at Piper and Jackson's or with the hands to relax and enjoy the end of the week, even if on a ranch, weekends were theoretical. Today, he wanted family.

"Hey, Piper, how're ya feeling sweetheart?" He kissed her cheek.

"Good, I only puke at seven and four now. So, if I sleep past seven, I miss the first round and if I am lucky enough to be in a sound nap at four, I often miss that one. However, today I was called in because the duplex I have ready to rent sprung a water leak."

"That's a bummer. Need help?" he asked as he grabbed a roll.

Piper slapped his hand. "Nope, the leak is fixed. But the fans won't finish drying the place for a few days. I have a mom and two children that needed to get in today, but I had to call her and tell her it would be a few more days."

Jackson gave Sawyer a beer and asked. "Anyone I know?"

"Maybe but I need to get dinner finished because your baby bump is hungry and so is his mama."

"All right. I'm happy to help if you need it," offered Jackson.

"Nope, I have it. We'll eat in a few."

The men walked into the family room and relaxed, chatting about work when the doorknocker banged on the heavy front door timidly.

"I'll get it. I know who it is," yelled Piper. When she came back into the room, both men had their boots off and their feet on the table, joking around. "Jackson Carter Knight, Sawyer Elijah Knight, get your feet off my leather covered coffee table."

Both men jerked their feet off the table. "What are you on about woman? You never cared before."

"Piper, I'm sorry." Sawyer leaned over to Jackson speaking in a stage whisper, "Must be hormones, man. Just go with it." Jackson's answer was to raise his eyebrows in reproach.

"Sawyer, this is..." Piper's voice faded off when Sawyer turned his head just as a small powerhouse raced to him.

"Are you my daddy?"

Cami grabbed up Lily and looked on helplessly as her son went on to tell his 'whole' name. He then informed the two stunned gentlemen all about the similarities between himself and his daddy. Sawyer and Jackson looked over the top of the boy's head in Camille's direction, but Cami only had eyes for Sawyer. He lifted his shell-shocked face and raised an eyebrow in question. Cami bit her lip so hard Sawyer was afraid she'd break the skin. It was her tell when she was deep in the middle of trouble. Sweet Jesus, she looked beautiful. His gut seized.

He continued to stare at her and finally, she nodded. He quickly glanced at the little girl in her arms then back at the boy. His son. How could that be? Camille had left him close to six years ago. Five years and eight months ago, to be exact. He thought he'd quit counting. It meant Eli's birthday must have just passed.

Eli had quit chatting and was waiting for Sawyer to answer him. Jackson said, "You sure look like alike, don't you?"

It was true. Little Eli was the spitting image of Sawyer's own childhood pictures. Five, that's what he'd said. And Lily, obviously his little sister, was four. He turned back to Cami and tears were racing down her cheeks.

"Eli, honey, we need to go. Tell the men it was nice meeting them and—"

"No!" thundered Sawyer. He pinned Camille with his gaze blazing with so many things, she took a step back. He grabbed Eli whose lip was trembling, tears filling his eyes, and hugged him tight. His own tears choked his words as overwhelming emotion thickened his tongue. He had a son. One he never knew he had. Anger wove amongst the riot of emotions he was experiencing. He had to tone it down. Pull it together. But hell. A son!

Sawyer sat Eli on his lap and used his thumb to wipe the tears from his face. "Yes, Eli, I'm your daddy. I'm very proud to meet you."

Piper had sat Cami on a chair with Lily tightly attached to her. The image of a spider monkey crossed his mind drawing a small smile from him. Much to his relief and Camille's obvious distress, Piper served dinner in the family room. "Are you hungry, Eli?"

"No, sir, I ate. Mama said we shouldn't go to someone's house hungry."

"Well, this isn't just any old person's house, it's Uncle Jackson and Aunt Piper's house. They don't care if you come hungry. I'm sure Aunt Piper has some dessert in that gigantic kitchen of hers."

Eli simply nodded but didn't take any food. "Me and Lily ate but mama didn't, so maybe she can eat."

Good boy. Taking care of his mama. He returned his gaze to Cami. She did look pale, thinner than he remembered her, but her breasts were fuller, her hips wider. He was shocked at the old feelings jumping at him. His emotions were all over the place but taking care of her was as natural as breathing.

"Camille, is that true?"

She shivered as she once did when he used that tone. It was an unconscious method he'd used to gain compliance when he expected her to balk at his direction. A part of him was just as connected to her as he'd been before she left. She must've felt it too.

"I ate today," she said with a bite of attitude. He loved that about her. Sassy to the end.

"If not dinner, lunch?" When she didn't answer, he sat his son on the couch next to him and dropped a kiss on his soft hair before standing to walk over to Camille. He reached for Lily who had begun to take a deep interest in the new man in her brother's life.

"Are the rumors true?"

"I have no idea. Rumors are usually not told to the person being chatted about." His lips twitched at her prim answer. He should be flaming mad at her, and maybe he would be later, but right now, all he could be is hopeful in his frustration. He nodded, trying to be satisfied.

Piper spoke up. "The bad ones, no, the ex, yes, but there is so much more you need to hear. You have no idea."

Sawyer continued to stare into Camille's eyes as he reached for Lily again. "Lily for Camilly?"

"Piccadilly, really."

He did smile then. He had called Camille, Camilly Piccadilly their whole lives. "Nice. Am I jumping a claim if I stake ownership of this beauty as well?"

Camille shook her head. "No. She has your last name."

That did surprise him, but it served his purpose. Presumptuous or not, he now had two children to call him daddy and he liked that. He liked it a lot. "Well, Miss Lily, do you want to sit in Daddy's lap while Mama eats her dinner?"

"Oh, but I'm not..." her words faded to nothing as he gave her the look he knew she remembered. He had paddled her rear a few times in their last year of dating after she had turned eighteen and could really consent.

"Do I need to make you a plate, Camille?"

His voice was well modulated but with considerable effort that obviously wasn't missed by Camille if the biting of her lip and the answering spark in her eyes were any indication. He had the urge to paddle that beautiful, rounded ass and take over her care immediately. Piper implied the gossip was what it always was, false, but still, where there's smoke, there had to be a little fire. He'd find out the whole story but not tonight. His girl looked exhausted, as exhausted as he suddenly felt. He softened his voice. No matter what happened after this, he had his son and she had all but told him he could be Lily's daddy as well. Children needed their mother and he needed her too.

"Sawyer..."

"Eat something. You need your strength."

His voice was firm and gentle. At least that was what he was going for with her tonight. Her attempt at a smile fell flat, but she nodded and put some food on her plate showing little interest in what she added. He knew she didn't like the Brussels sprouts she had placed on her plate.

Cami looked up at him with some hope, as though she had thought of something she could do for him, something he'd accept. Maybe it was because she missed him, because she was tired, and he naturally took over with her. It was equally possible it was because he hadn't dressed her down for showing up unannounced after leaving without talking to him. Whatever it was, he wanted to give it to her for now.

Her words were tentative. "Can I serve you?"

She nodded at Lily in his lap and Eli who had yet to fall silent for more than a few moments. The question was innocent, but his cock did a somersault in anticipation of her meaning. The silence was only interrupted by Eli asking his newly acquired aunt if he could have more milk. Sawyer tried to take the emphasis off her–them, and back on the children, the situation. He felt hope rising in his chest at her words. He must have stared too long because her cheeks blushed.

"I mean, would you like me to make you a plate?"

"Please." She smiled then. Still lacking in genuine joy but much better than the first one she'd tried. For now, he'd take it. He leaned back and watch Camille. There were differences but she was holding her own. *That's my girl. We'll figure this out.*

Chapter 4

Eli, despite his earlier exuberance, seemed a little leery of his father, now that he'd found him. Lily had no such reticence. Cami was hesitant but put on a good face. Sawyer looked inward and admitted his whole life had turned upside down in a few minutes and the longer he sat in this family room, the more tangled and frantic his thoughts became.

On the one hand, it was so simple. Take the family in front of him and live happily ever after. On the other hand, there was too much that had happened not to tease it all out and put things to right, however they could. Then and only then should they consider their next steps. Life had suddenly gotten very interesting.

And then there was Piper. He needed to have a firm conversation with his sister-in-law and the part she played in all of this. Suddenly, his hand itched. A lot. He looked over at his brother who had been chatting with Eli when he could get a word in edge wise and saw the way he looked at his wife occasionally. Jackson's brat meter was blaring as loudly as his own, alerting them to not one naughty woman but two. Maybe he'd let Jackson handle Piper. Sawyer had enough on his plate trying to learn the children and watch out for their mother as much as she allowed while wading through the quagmire that was now his life.

Jackson lifted his head after coaxing a piece of cake into Lily's mouth to look in his brother's direction. Sawyer knew what he must have been thinking because if the situation were reversed, he'd have thought the same thing. Be careful. You were hurt once, and you don't know the situation so go slow. You don't even know that Eli is yours. But he did. The boy was the spitting image of him at his age. He gave his brother a nod in understanding and Jackson, good man that he was, accepted it.

Piper spoke into one of the uncomfortable lulls in adult conversation. "I need to run into Austin in the morning, but I'll be back before dinner. I told Camille if it was too uncomfortable staying with her parents, given the situation with them, she could stay with us. You know, until the floors are dry in the duplex. She's taking one of them."

Piper ran a small but important global investment firm mostly from town. In addition to the co-administering of both ranches, she recently had added landlord to her list of ways to fill a day. Sawyer was more than impressed with the abilities of Jackson's woman but there was no way in hell Camille was staying with Piper when she and the kids could stay with him. Should stay with him. His inner voice tried to protect his heart, cautioning him she had left before but now, he had a son. He'd been a sorry excuse of a man these last years since she had left town, left him. He'd find out what the whole story was and deal with the issue as it became clearer to him. Until then, they were his.

God help him, it might not matter if she had done it all for a selfish reason, he couldn't imagine living his life without her any longer. Not now that he had her in front of him. He'd done that and was miserable. He'd make her see him as her lover again. Then, as her husband. In fact, he wanted to marry her tomorrow but knew it was foolish. Watching the young woman his sassy girl had become, he knew she'd want more than a fast wedding. She had changed so much in some ways and not at all in others. But tonight, regardless of what had gone before or because of it, she would agree with him and stay at the Clear Knight.

"Oh, I think we'll be fine, Piper. In fact, we should get back before my parents go to bed." Camille began to pick up her plate and started to clear away the other dishes. Jackson's big hand covered hers.

"Don't worry, honey, I'll get this handled after you all go to the ranch." His meaning was clear. Go home with Sawyer and figure this out.

"Why do you have to get there before they go to bed? Was it because you would have stayed here but have now changed your mind?" asked Sawyer.

She was meek, too meek. There was a lot going on her and her sad shrug wasn't going to cut it. Sawyer was giving no quarter and knew she wouldn't ask for any. Cami didn't answer as she continued to gather her bag and reached for Lily. Sawyer was not playing any games with Camille nor was he going to keep his thoughts to himself. He'd call her on anything he felt needed to be addressed. He pushed the point with her.

"Don't you have a key to the house?" he asked.

Something wasn't right and his protective vibes were clanging. She was his woman, yes, his. He still claimed her no matter what had happened in the past. He was the most complete he had been since he got her message and found out she was gone.

She stared into his eyes acting as though she had been caught in a naughty act and didn't want to admit it but didn't want to lie. His feelings for her were so intense they hurt.

"Cami?"

She replied quietly, "No one calls me that anymore."

"Except me. Stop avoiding my questions."

Her heavy sigh rang out. "I had a difference of opinion with my mother today and she said she didn't want to risk the wrong people getting access to her home. So, no key. Her implications were clear."

"The hell she did!" The words rolled out like thunder in a storm.

"Daddy," two little voices chastised, "that's a bad word." He grinned at the sound of being called daddy and quickly apologized. Fuck. Things were definitely changing. Returning his attention to Cami, he sobered. Sawyer hadn't missed the hitch in her voice or the trembling lip she was biting. He reached out and pulled it from between her teeth as he had countless times before and she let him like she had done countless times before.

Leaning in, he commanded in a low voice next to her ear, "We're going to the ranch, little girl. This daddy is taking care of all his little ones, starting now."

CAMILLE'S EYES OPENED wide as she processed what Sawyer had said. He remembered. She'd been frustrated with him and called him 'daddy' after one of his especially domineering days. She had been playing around, but he liked it and so did she. That had been the first time he'd spanked her for doing something dumb and then sassing him over it.

It was a game, but she had fallen further in love with him that very afternoon. And like that far distant day, tonight her tummy rolled, her sex tingled and ached when she heard him refer to it. She wanted to submit to his demands, no, not submit, offer her troubles for him to carry awhile. Sawyer would take those troubles and still demand her submission. Could she do that?

"But what about your brother?"

"Walker? It's a big house, honey. A big, too quiet, house. He's gone until Monday morning and he'll love his niece and nephew living with him. Besides, we have a lot of things to talk about. Better to do that in private after the children have been put to bed. Little missy here is dozing off now." He looked over at his son and indicated Eli with a nod of his head. "He isn't far behind."

"Okay but we are not 'living' with you. We're staying until we can move into the duplex. A few days."

His only response was to grunt. Her whole lower half tingled. Damn she has missed him. Sawyer put his boots on while holding onto Lily draped over his shoulder. He grinned when the four-year-old snored softly. He was so strong, so capable. She hadn't had either since she left him behind five and a half years earlier. He reached for his Stetson.

"We'll talk about it. Later."

"No. We aren't going unless you agree."

She had to keep some control. Lord knew it took nothing to bow to his dominance. She'd been a pushover when younger but since having her children, she could be like a lioness with her cubs if necessary. She needed even footing or at least a say in how things would go.

"I'll agree for the moment, but you need to know that while little bit here might not be mine legally, bigger bit is, and I plan on him living with me on the ranch. It'd be nice if he could have everyone, but I'm willing to work out an arrangement if that is unacceptable to you."

She heard the hardness in his voice, the steel in his words. She doubted he meant to take him from her. Sawyer had grown up without his mom a lot of his childhood and she knew he'd felt that loss deeply. If push came to shove, he'd work things out. Right now, looking at his piercing blue eyes and squared jaw, she wouldn't stake her life on it. Besides she owed him this time.

She was tired. Who would have figured she'd go from no one wanting her children to fighting to keep them with her? Maybe coming back wasn't the right choice. Even as the thought appeared, she knew it was wrong. She needed to come back, sink down roots for the children, and share Eli with his father. She must have taken too long for Sawyer leaned in again.

"Get a move on, baby. My hand is itching, and I expect you haven't had a real spanking since I last gave you one. I'm thinking you need one pretty badly right about now. I had intended on waiting until you gave me the whole sorry tale of what happened since you were last in my arms, however I could be persuaded to start off with lighting up your backside. Is that what you want or are you going to mind Daddy?"

She was positively wet. She hadn't been turned on since, well, since Sawyer. Lord in heaven, she missed this, missed him. "Thanks for the offer, Piper but I guess Sawyer is right, they do need time to bond before school and work start for us.

"If you're sure. If this Knight man gets too much to deal with, you can come back here."

"Honey, I don't think we should interfere," said Jackson as he looked at Sawyer heading for the door.

"Whatever. I know you guys. Too much for polite company sometimes and definitely too much for stressed women. I meant what I said, Camille."

"Thanks. Now promise you won't forget to call me the moment the place is dry."

"I'll call." Cami noticed she forgot to say the rest but there wasn't any use in pushing the point. She had bigger fish to fry this weekend.

Chapter 5

S awyer led Cami and the kids back to the Clear Knight. Eli had thrown a fit when she wouldn't let him ride with Sawyer without a car seat. Lily, seeing her brother's display, decided she would join the party. Camille looked about ready to cry. Sawyer saw his baby was hanging on by a thread. Eli must have sensed she was feeling weak and went for the jugular.

"I need my daddy," he demanded. Lily added a screech to announce her disagreement of the mama decision as well.

Sawyer saw the opportunity to educate how things would be going from here on out. He gentled his boss man voice but kept enough authority in it to get the children's attention.

"Son, I do not appreciate you speaking to your mother that way and it will not happen again. Do you understand me? A man, no matter his age, is respectful of women, their mother especially. Apologize and I'll take you to see my horses tomorrow. Continue being naughty and you might not see any of the ranch all day."

That did the trick as he had hoped it would. He was winging it after all. Eli jumped into the booster seat and assisted his mother in snapping him in. Sawyer thought the boy was too big for a baby seat, but he didn't know about these things enough to venture an opinion. He turned to Lily and that little one had

43

already gone back to sleep. Well, good enough then. She was so much like her mother; his heart ached for her, for them all.

"But, Daddy," Eli sniffled quietly. "I wanted to ride with you because I just found you." Damn, he was good. Sawyer was instantly down on his haunches, reaching for his son's hand.

"And we will see each other every day. You won't ever have to look for me again because you'll know just where I am."

"Promise?"

"Promise." The sniffle he heard from the front seat softened his heart. Yeah, this was his family now and come hell or high water, he would be leading the way from now on.

He didn't have any half beds at the ranch but there were plenty of bedrooms. Camille decided they would do best in the same queen-size bed in Jackson's old room. It was next to Sawyer's big bedroom.

"I'll sleep with them, so they aren't scared when they wake up."

"I want to say no but I understand for tonight. Tomorrow, we're going to examine how things should go. You get them settled in," his deeper voice sounding omnipresent in the bedroom, "but it's still early. I don't need to know everything tonight, Cami, but I do need to know some things. I've waited a long time and I think I deserve some answers up front."

After the children were down, he led Camille into the kitchen where he started rummaging in the refrigerator and pulling out a pie. Next, he started a pot of coffee and listened to some filler information Cami was sharing. She was a nurse and was starting as the school district nurse in a few weeks. Good, she intended to stay. That fixed one potential problem.

She had lived in Nevada the first six months of her marriage and just before she was due to deliver, she moved to Alaska. She came from there to here, arriving yesterday. He knew she was leaving a lifetime out of the outline, but it gave him a reference framework.

Taking their coffee and allowing her to carry their pie, they ended at the big country dining table. After a swig of coffee and a bite of pie, he put his fork down and watched her for a few moments. "Time to fill in the blanks before Eli was born, baby."

She nodded and took a drink of her coffee setting it down with grim determination. "Okay. Remember I was working at Hanson's drug store and had taken on tutoring the sports teams' players in math and science to make extra money while you were off rodeoing?"

"Yes, we were trying to get together as much money as we could before we got married." He knew it was a low blow to highlight their plans that she ran from, but he couldn't help it.

She hesitated. "Right. It was your last year at college because you had taken a max load. I couldn't afford college, but we thought it didn't matter since we were going to work and live on the ranch. Anyway, one of the boys I was tutoring was the son of an attorney in the next town, same last name as me."

Sawyer nodded and waited. They had joked about that fact at the time. He had to check his overwhelming urge to stop what he could see was a hard retelling but if he was going to get to the bottom of things, he had to let her go at her own pace, no matter how excruciating it was to him. She would get through it.

Knowing his girl for more than half her life, he knew the basics about her. She hated being interrupted, but she had no such compunction for her own behavior. Then having Piper as a sister-in-law had taught him even more about women. Even Josie and Walker, tiptoeing through the rubble though they were, were good for some additional lessons in how women think. He was still on shaky ground. Therefore, he waited on Camille.

"Well, I guess he was an important attorney because when a traveling lawyer saw me joking with my student's father, he took it as more than it was. Like, since the last names were the same, I was related. He joined the conversation for a few moments and when it started to rain, offered me a ride home." She shuddered with the memory. "I thought it was a safe thing to do. It wasn't."

"What the fuck is his name?" Sawyer stood in anger and frustration. He wanted to find the man who had hurt his girl and break his neck after he did a few more things like drag him behind his horse for a start.

"Sawyer... Daddy, please."

The hitch in her voice did him in. She cut him to the quick. That and the reference to the part of him that would do anything to make her happy. He stopped and scooped her up in his arms. She stiffened and then relaxed in his sudden hold. The tears were slipping silently down her face and it cut him like a knife.

His anger felt somewhat appeased, diffused momentarily in action. Walking with her in his arms felt even better. He sat her on the sofa while he lit the kindling on the fire, steepling three small logs over the top of the starter. He gathered her back into his arms. Settling her hips and thighs between his legs on the sofa, they faced the flames.

"Go on, honey. Let's get it all out so we don't have to go back there again." She nodded but was silent. Finally, he prompted gruffer than he wanted but it was the most controlled he could be. "What happened on your way home with this man, baby?"

"Aiden. His name is Aiden Blevins. He forced himself on me so quickly, I had hardly any time to think before he was... in. I promise I didn't agree or even know until it was too late. I fought, but it was almost after the fact. He laughed."

In a million years, he wouldn't have thought that. She never told him. He was her protector. Her confidante, and she had never told him. Maybe he had thought they were closer than they were. Or maybe she blamed him for being so far away from her when it happened. He shouldn't have been.

"How bad?"

"What?"

"How bad did he hurt you, Camille?"

"Physically, not badly because you and I had, well, you know it wasn't my first time. But emotionally, and mentally, it devastated me."

"Why didn't you tell me? We were going to get married."

"Don't you see? That's part of the reason why. You were gone to the rodeo and had barely made it back for your final weeks of classes before graduation. You know how busy you were. And it was important that you finished. I couldn't do that to you. Not when you were so close to the end. I did try to tell my mom, but she said I got in his car so I must have known what was going to happen."

What could he say? He was supposed to protect her, and he hadn't. But her mother? He could hardly comprehend the devastation to his girl. "And your father?"

"He didn't know. I didn't ever tell anyone else for a long time."

He couldn't get his head around this. "How about after I graduated?"

"Remember, I was young. My dad let my mom raise us kids because he worked long hours to feed the five of us. You kept me more sheltered than most girls in so many ways. You stood between me and the seedier part of life by keeping me out here or busy with our life goals."

"When I came back?"

She shook her head. "By the time you graduated and had finished with your next rodeo, it had been a month and by then, I was vomiting."

"You were pregnant."

"Yes, and I thought it was from the rape. I wasn't positive, but it seemed likely, so I told my mother. She said I didn't have any choice, I had to marry the guy. She said I couldn't stay home. You had just gotten back. How could I tell you he raped me, and I was pregnant with his child? You wanted a child so badly. Besides, it was his word against mine. He was a new lawyer but considerably older and more experienced than me in everything."

"Of course, you could have told me. I had no reason not to believe you."

"I was ashamed, pushed out by my mother, and I believed he'd have tried to take the baby. She told him I was pregnant with his child. She told him she'd go to the police if he didn't marry me and she said she'd tell you if I refused. What else could I do?"

"You could have believed in me. In our love." He was so angry. She had taken away his baby and left their love. She didn't trust him or believe he could help.

"I was scared, confused, desperate. The last day I was in town I tried to call you, to talk to you, but I got your voice mail. I decided it was fate." Her voice faded in the memories. "I cried so much those first months."

The crying started then and all he could do was grapple with his own grief and questions as he tried to soothe her. He hugged, kissed and rocked his girl. Nothing felt so right as this. Behind them, a little voice spoke into the room.

"Why is Mama crying again? Isn't she happy?" Both adults startled.

Kissing Camille's temple, Sawyer methodically untangled himself from her, stood and scooped his son up into his arms. "Mommy is fine, son. What about you? Why are you up? Have a bad dream?"

"No, I'm thirsty and I don't know where the bathroom is here."

"Ah, yes, that is an important piece of information that I left out. Here. Let me get you to the bathroom down here and then we will get you a glass of juice."

"Water. Mama says you get bad teeth if you drink juice at night."

"And she's right. I forgot."

Bathroom and water taken care of, Sawyer took his son back upstairs. He showed him the hallway bathroom and tucked him in bed with his sister. Sawyer knew it was a little underhanded, but he wanted to know.

"Eli, does Mama cry a lot?"

"Sometimes when she thinks I'm asleep, I hear her. And she cried at Grandma's house because she was sad. Did you make her sad too?"

"No, son, we were just talking about sad things. Sometimes women just cry to feel better. I love you, and Lily, and Mama very much. I'll try to stop her from crying so much, okay? Let's work on making her happy."

"Okay." The little man nodded his head sagely. Sawyer loved him so much already.

Once downstairs, Sawyer found Camille sitting in the corner of the couch. Her tears had dried. Looking up into his eyes and watching warily as he sat next to her on the sofa, she nodded.

"Okay, just let me get the rest out while I can."

He nodded and took her hand in his. "Go ahead."

She told of the isolation, the declaration by the doctor that she was further along than she would have been if the child were Aiden's. She spoke of how he never touched her sexually after the rape until he raped her again. The last day he came home was when Eli was a few months old. He told her it wasn't rape because they were married.

"I believed him for a long time." She shrugged and sighed with the sad reality of her life at that time. She was glad he left to his girlfriend's permanently that same night. The one he eventually married. "Lily was conceived that night." Cami sat quietly then continued, "It was horrible, but it was how I got out of the situation. I found help, and I got what I wanted from the divorce. He promised to never contact me again or I can still bring charges against him.

"I thought it was time to come home. Eli needed his daddy. I had already given him your name in the divorce decree. I wanted to list you on his birth certificate, but they wouldn't let me because I was still married. Aiden had a DNA done to prove he wasn't the father. He did that soon after Elijah was born." She stopped but when he didn't say anything, she continued, "I had to prove I was unmarried at conception to get Aiden's name off the certificate. They couldn't put your name on the certificate without a paternity affidavit. At least they were able to remove Aiden's name. I didn't want Eli to go another day without knowing who he was, not that he cared at that stage. I also changed my name in the decree. So, when Lily was born, she took my name and I didn't have to list Aiden even though, ironically, he was her father. I'm sorry, Sawyer."

"I'm not. I'll call our attorney and he will get the right paperwork filed. I'll put my name on Eli's certificate. Now some people will probably know Lily isn't mine, but she looks like you with my blond hair. I don't imagine anyone will ask. I'll put my name on her certificate, if you want, but it's up to you."

"I think it's up to you." He heard the weariness in her words, the defeat in her tone.

"Then it's a matter of another affidavit. If you're sure."

She nodded. "Why would you do that? I mean, she is the product of rape, and is another man's child. Why do anything for us? I left you."

Sawyer thought about the question before answering. "Because I love you. I always have and after these last years trying to get on with my life without you, I know I always will. These are your children. Lily isn't to blame for her father. She belongs to you and Eli; Eli belongs to me. I hope you will belong to me as well, so why would I not add Lily to the whole and make us one unit? A family, with you. It's all I've ever wanted."

"How can you trust me after what I did?"

"Baby, all you did was believe what others told you. Things were done to you to make the path more winding than either of us planned, but you're stronger, more mature now, and won't let others take advantage again. Not easily, anyway. As far as trust? We will work on building it back up." Sawyer straightened. "What about this Aiden coming back to get her?"

"He doesn't know she exists and even if he did, he didn't want children and remember, I have the proof; I also left copies with the attorney and with the shelter. I took care of everything and he agreed not to contact us again."

"I always knew you were one smart cookie." He kissed her temple. "Would you be comfortable giving a copy to our attorney?"

She nodded. "Sawyer, it's been a long month. I'm overwhelmed, I'm tired. I'm going to bed."

"With me."

"No, with the kids."

"Listen, I'll compromise. You can sleep with the kids tonight as long as you know we do things my way now. You've had your time of running the show, keeping me out, taking my time with Eli from me. Now that I know the lay of the land, we have plenty to work out but Eli being in my daily life isn't something I will compromise on. So, either work with me or I take over completely. Your call."

Chapter 6

He was such an egotistical, pushy jerk. And she still loved him. She always had. On the one hand she was tempted to just let him have what he wanted, and she'd get a break. A break she hadn't had since she had climbed into that car with Aiden. Her stress level had been uncontrollable until she had gotten her divorce and then a new stress started. Survival.

On the other hand, her feelings and his natural dominance didn't negate the fact that she needed more control. She had learned never to abdicate all of one's control. He thought he could tell her what to do, and she'd just roll over. He needed to know that isn't how things worked any longer, even if it was easier for both of them. Her independence was hard earned.

She wasn't just some innocent teenager who enjoyed submitting to her bossy man. She was a woman who had fought her way to where she was and by all that was sacred, she was not giving in to another man. Even if she couldn't help but love him more for taking the children, no questions asked. It was still pitching her ballgame.

She told him just that. He didn't say she was wrong, or that he was going to change his way of dealing with the situation she had laid at his feet. He didn't say she was right or that he understood her need to be in control of the children and her destiny. He said very little in fact.

As she followed him around, closing things up, picking up their plates, rinsing them off and putting them in the dishwasher, she continued to declare her sovereignty, even though this ritual was so familiar to her. How easy it would be not to fight any longer.

When they walked up the staircase to the bedrooms, she wondered if he had even heard her. Once on the landing, he turned, pinning her to the wall and kissed her deeply. His tongue fought for entry and their tongues dueled for supremacy outside the children's bedroom door. His knee settled between her thighs and claimed that spot, further pinning her. He rubbed his thigh against her core and she moaned.

Her resolve was fading and her need to be made love to by Sawyer, a man who loved her, was almost suffocating. Then he stepped away and smiled gently before dropping a quick kiss on her softened lips. He caressed her cheek, tweaked her protruding nipples. His smile turned salacious.

He tucked her hair behind her ear and said, "Tonight only." Without another word, he turned to the room beside them and entered, closing the door softly.

He'd really left her standing in all her achy need. He teased her, made love to her lips, held her close and left her standing. Unfulfilled. Empty. Even more amazing was that he ignored his own needs after playing to them. This Sawyer was more mature than the one she had left six years ago. The one she had left never passed up an opportunity to come inside her. Stake his claim. Feed their needs. No, this one was even more in control than the younger one had ever been.

He'd left her needy on purpose. He knew what he was doing and how much it challenged her to stick to her guns. He didn't lock the door to his room. In fact, she wasn't sure it was completely closed.

Camille was more in control as well. She had been through a lot of heartache and loss. She'd worked damn hard to get where she was. But now that she was at the place she had fought to be, could she handle the new and improved Sawyer? That man she had left almost standing at the alter and who, by all intents and purposes was not going to allow that to happen again?

It's what you wanted. It's what you said you were going to do. It has turned out like you hoped. With one exception. She had hoped to do this from a safe distance. Far enough away that she could protect her heart if she needed to, build the relationship before risking her heart. That wasn't happening according to plan. Her heart and his, it seemed, had never been disengaged.

She walked into the bedroom and closed the door. She considered locking it but if the children needed the bathroom, they wouldn't be able to get out. Sawyer had brought in their bags. Her other clothes would arrive any day. She had sent things to Seattle on the barge and then had them sent in a POD storage container. She should get the call any day.

As she lay in bed, she thought of her life since she left home. She'd dreamed he would accept Eli, Lily, and herself and now that it seemed to have happened, she was leery that it was so easy. Even after looking at all the angles and finishing her best planning, Camille wasn't naïve to think things would be easy.

Sawyer had loved her but he was never an easy man. Her eyes were full of teenage love but even then, she'd know there was an intense man underneath the lover he presented to her.

He would want certain concessions that she was not sure she was able to give him. She could compromise because she'd need his help to make things work here but there would be compromising on both sides.

Her hometown was full of gossip and speculation about people's lives. Her mother would never be happy with the fact that she was back with Sawyer. Or that the children had his last name. She wasn't going to inform her mother of anything she didn't have to because that is how they both wanted it. Her mother could declare deniable plausibility and in a way, after Camille was forced out of town with Aiden, it was predominately true. It was the way Camille needed it.

Cami wondered if Carla Hendrix had ever felt bad for forcing her daughter into a marriage she didn't want. Away from the man she wanted. If Camille was being totally honest, she had been ashamed and fearful of rejection. It wasn't something she could have borne. At that time of their lives, Sawyer was headstrong and jumped in feet first. The reasoning often came later, but equally as often it was too late to remedy any of his mistakes, so he built around them. Such as the night Eli was conceived.

They had both been very careful to use protection before sex. Sawyer didn't like Camille using chemicals and that included a daily pill. She offered to get a different type of birth control from the doctor, but he didn't want her mother finding out. Camille told him she could be discreet and that she was nineteen and had graduated from high school. Old enough to make her own reproductive and sexual choices.

Ultimately, she hadn't taken birth control of any kind but did use a sponge insert. It had worked well. Sawyer was never squeamish so when he wanted to have sex and she was in her time of the month, he took her anyway. They came together fast, furious and without protection. She had assured him that since she was on her period, nothing would take.

"Don't worry, Sawyer, I know about these things."

But she hadn't and when she was raped several weeks later, and sick weeks after that, she thought it was from the rape. She was happy when it was discovered to be Sawyer's but then mortified that she hadn't told him or gone into the doctor to get more information. None of this would have happened if she had been more responsible.

She mentally shook her head. It didn't matter now. All things happened for a reason and Cami now had a career, her children were past babyhood, barely, and Sawyer wanted his son. He'd even accepted Lily as part of the package. What more could she want?

Camille knew what else she wanted but on her terms: new, renegotiated terms. Her old way of allowing Sawyer to lead and obediently following him wouldn't work now. But she was tired, and it would be so easy to do just that. His scent overwhelmed her senses when he had pulled her close tonight. The scent she had in her memory but couldn't quite touch before tonight came back strong and clear. It was comforting and powerful, soothing her frayed nerves and still she couldn't sleep, even though she was exhausted in every way.

Before she understood what her mind was directing, she had crawled out of the bed again, grabbed her pillow and padded to Sawyer's bedroom. He hadn't closed the door completely. With children, that could be risky if he still slept as she remembered. Naked. Taking a deep breath, she pushed the door open. She stood watching him. He was on his side, facing away from her. His butt covered in pajama bottoms.

All she wanted was a pillow. She'd leave hers on his bed and grab one of his, just to help her sleep. His scent relaxed her, and she just knew that if she had that scent surrounding her, she'd sleep like a baby. Reaching for the pillow lying next to him, a large, work roughened hand grabbed her wrist. Turning to face her, he rubbed his tired face.

"What's wrong, baby girl? Do you want to crawl in with your daddy? I can cuddle you."

She almost cried. He couldn't know how many nights she had tried to conjure up the times he had called her baby girl. Whether it was loving, correcting, or protecting, it was his signature 'I love you' phrase. She stood and stared at him as her pulse heated and her sex wept with joyful arousal.

"I-I was having a hard time sleeping and..." She shrugged, indicating the pillow she was going to exchange. "I thought I would trade." Her belly flipped in the closeness. Tears burned her nose and brimmed in her eyes. She had to get control of her overwhelming need for him. She sniffed hard. "Never mind." Turning, she forgot he held her wrist. The tug of steel reminded her she was tethered to him in more than a physical way. He pulled her towards him.

"Crawl in, baby. I'll just hold you."

She shook her head. "The children."

"What about them? Honey, we are just going to cuddle and sleep. I don't intend on doing more than that no matter how much I want to. We have to take this slow and as we do it will serve many purposes. It will help address my fear of being hurt again, you will learn to lean on someone else again, and the kids, well, they will learn it is how adults who love each other act."

She wanted to say she didn't love him, but she couldn't lie. That was her one deal with herself. No more lying. She still loved him, but the accountability wasn't something she'd be able to give to another. She had to remain in control no matter how much she longed for his brand of love. His kind of dominance. Tonight, though, she desperately needed sleep.

She hadn't had a good night's sleep in weeks. He tugged again. This time she let him bring her onto the bed. He settled her in the warmth and security of his scent surrounding her, dragging the blanket over her and wrapping his arm around her. Pulling her tight to him, he kissed her cheek.

"Sleep, baby. We'll work this out a little at a time." She nodded and fell quickly asleep.

Chapter 7

Life was busy. The last week was full of negotiations, compromises and arguments. She hadn't realized how quickly Sawyer worked but he had her signing the affidavit for the birth certificates in his attorney's office Monday afternoon. Sawyer worked but took Eli with him, which made Lily cry and Camille worry, which showed itself in anger.

"This isn't going to work," she declared.

He crossed his arms. "We are not going to argue over this."

"You're right, we aren't. I'm taking that duplex and you can see Eli whenever you want."

"Camille, what are you afraid of, baby?"

"I don't want them hurt."

"Or yourself if I'm reading this right. I don't want to hurt either and it isn't my plan, I promise you. I only took Eli today because he is a bit older and I can only keep my eye on one at a time while still getting work done. I'll take Lily but when I'm not working. They need to learn what living on a ranch is like before I can trust them to be safe. You know I'm right. I refuse to risk their safety."

Camille nodded. She sighed and her silent tears made another appearance. They had arrived often in the days since she had come to the ranch. Hell, since she had left it.

"I know, but I hate for Lily to feel left out."

"Honey, she's little and newsflash, there will always be times that the youngest will feel left out. I'll take her when it's safe, and before you even insinuate it, when and where I take her has nothing to do with who her biological father is and everything to do with age and safety. Our little ones won't be with me if I can't keep a good eye on them until they are older."

She heard the 'our' in his description and while she melted at his words, she remembered how it was in his dominant nature to take over. Not this time. Not until she was more than ready and even then, it would be a cooperative partnership.

"Right. Okay, I agree it has to be safe. Right now, I have to sign the papers for the duplex and get the utilities turned on. I'll take Lily with me if you can keep an eye on Eli. I'll come and gather our things after I get back. Hopefully, we can move in tonight."

"Are you willing to only visit your son? Because I refuse to be without him every day."

"Sorry, buster, but I have sole custody. I got it in the divorce. I retain control in their lives against all comers. Even you. I told you no one is going to take over my life. If I invite someone in, it will be on my terms."

"Camille. Stop and think for a moment. There's plenty of room here. The kids can each have their own room or share if they are more comfortable. I work a ranch that doesn't have regular hours and running into town every time I want the kids to experience something isn't feasible. What can I do to keep you from leaving? I want to see the kids every day and if we are working on our relationship, rebuilding it, and if I am to work on being a good father, I need that."

"You can't ask me to change my plans for you. Sawyer, it's not fair."

"Sometimes I work long hours and all the free time I can get during the day is meals. Even if all I can get with them is at breakfast and dinner, it is more than I would if you were in town." He stepped closer and lifted her chin. "Please, baby girl. Help me get this right."

His look was so earnest. She could use someone to bounce off her ideas about the kids and sleeping in his bed, no sex, had been incredible the last few nights. She wanted more but that would come later. For now, it was all she could handle, and Sawyer seemed to have accepted that, even though he got her riled up sexually whenever he got half a chance. She loved that he was giving her space, and she needed to be as giving as he was trying to be.

"Okay."

"Yeah? Great. I'll call Piper."

"No, I'll call Piper. You know I start work the day before the kids start school. That is Monday. I had thought to let Mom watch the kids on that day but since I came out here, she has been avoiding me."

"It's the guilt. I'm sure of it. Give her some time and act as though there isn't any problem between you." Camille opened her mouth to speak only to have his index finger lay across her lips. "Shush, baby. I know it isn't easy, so all I'm saying is don't avoid her. Things have a way of working out."

"Maybe. You know I don't like bossy men anymore, right?"

"Oh, I have a feeling you like this one just fine. You're out of practice. That's all. We both are. Slow and easy, remember?"

She watched Sawyer wrangle with something and ultimately, he blurted it out. "Cami, are you sure you need to work?"

"Oh, yeah. If I don't, especially in the first months, we will fight every day."

"I've missed your sassiness." His smile told her he wasn't lying. "And I still know how to handle a mouthy miss."

"No spanking." Camille wanted her tone to be as serious as it could get. She wasn't a young adult who needed the boundaries, she was a full grown, mother of two. A woman with a career and no need for spankings.

"You need your daddy, though. And he needs you."

He pulled her in for a light kiss and a comforting hug. His arms wrapped around her, drawing her tight to his firm body. She could have pointed out she had done just fine without him, but the reality was she had survived, not flourished, giving it all to school, work, and her children. She didn't begrudge any of it and still, there were days she longed for what Sawyer Knight offered: to be the one taken care of at the end of the day.

Sawyer's comforting ways and calm steady voice was like coming home.

She'd simply need to avoid giving him a reason to think she deserved a spanking. It could be done even if they always made her hot as hell. She couldn't have sex right now. That day would come and if things went as her dreams always ended, it would be Sawyer sharing the experience with her. Time would tell.

Walker had gone to Austin again this weekend and was due back on Monday morning, early. Evidently, Josie, the woman he was wooing at present, had been Walker's girlfriend and an employee of Piper's over a year ago. Then, when people were shot on the Clearwater Ranch, Piper had gone rogue, and the Knight men were in full protective—and likely spanking—mode. The combination had been too much, and Josie had said enough.

She'd gone back to the corporate offices in Austin, but ultimately, when Walker had tried to reignite their spark, she decided it would only have a chance if she wasn't part of Piper's dominion. They still got along, but whatever worked for them is what they should do. Piper was bummed, she told Camille over lunch last week, but now she could see her point. It had taken some stress off their relationship as well as Josie and Walker's.

"Hey, I'm sorry I left you in the lurch over that duplex," Camille told Piper as they made the sides to go with the beef the men were cooking on the grill.

"Nah, I've already rented it out. Are you okay with being at the ranch with Sawyer and Walker?"

"I hardly see Walker during the week, and he's gone from Friday afternoon until Monday morning, so I only saw him at dinner a few days last week and the guys were working long hours."

"Yeah, it's that time of year. In about six weeks, things will slow down and then they get underfoot."

"Well, Walker is a sweetheart as always. Bossy as the Knight boys have always been, but just asked a few questions, said it was ultimately our decision. He thanked me for bringing the kids home. That's it. Lily has fallen in love with the new men in her life and Eli, well, he needs the examples on how to be a man. He doesn't always like it but..." she shrugged. "It isn't me he gets mad at now."

"Oh, I think Sawyer can handle things pretty well."

"But he's a pushover."

"He is falling in love with his family. Things will settle down and get real sooner than you think."

On cue, Lily came running into the kitchen, crying. Camille picked her up and tried to get her to calm down enough to understand what was wrong. All she could get was the word 'day' and 'no'. Eli followed her into the kitchen.

"What is wrong with your sister?"

Elijah graced the room with his dramatic sigh. "Daddy told her no."

Piper mumbled under her breath loud enough for Camille to barely hear over the renewed wounded cries of her daughter. "Let him handle it."

Cami ignored her new best friend. "Hush, Lily, you're okay." She looked at her son. "Why did he tell her no?"

Eli shrugged and turned from the room. "Something about fire. You know how girls are."

Camille opened her mouth to respond to that rude statement when Sawyer stepped in the way to block the boy's exit. "Elijah Knight, what did I tell you about being rude?" His voice did not rise above normal range, but his disapproval screamed loudly.

The boy's shoulders drooped. "A man takes care of the women in his life. A gentleman rancher is never rude."

"That's right." He turned his son around to face the females in the kitchen. "You know what to do."

"Yes, sir. Sorry, Mom. Sorry, Lily. Sorry, Auntie Piper."

"Aw, honey," started Camille but Sawyer put his hand up to halt her words. He met her look of incredulity with his raised eyebrow. "Sawyer..."

"Cami, do you and I need to take a walk to discuss the matter?" Camille wasn't sure he was actually offering conversation or if it was code for his hand doing the talking on her butt, so she shook her head. "Good. Now, give me Lily."

"I've got her."

"And now I'm going to have her." He put his arms out and took the now sniffling but otherwise quiet, four-year-old. "Lily was playing around the grill with a ball. I told her she couldn't play too close to the fire. She had a tough time listening and finally, after moving her several times, I took the ball."

"Oh." Camille felt deflated. She had been the only protector for her children. Letting Sawyer in was harder than she thought.

"Now, Miss Piccadilly and I are going to talk about how to listen."

"She's only four."

"Yep, but she was plenty old enough to ignore me when I told her to stop doing something. She has to learn to mind, Camille. Life is too dangerous otherwise."

His look and tone told her he was testing her as well. Could she allow him to father the children or would she be in line for her own discipline? She watched Lily lay her head on his shoulder. The children were having fewer adjustment issues than she was. She'd been getting her own way more than they were and she worried that Sawyer might take her to task in a more profound way than he had corrected the children's behaviors.

She nodded.

"Good girl." He leaned down and kissed her on the lips.

"Me, too, Daddy." He kissed Lily's cheek. "No, here." She pointed to her lips.

"Sorry, sweetheart. Lips are for mommies." He kissed her cheek again.

She nodded. "Oh."

Crisis avoided; dinner went without any further dramatics. As the women were cleaning up the dishes, Piper observed, "He's a natural. I wasn't sure how it would work because he has been closed off for the last few years."

"I know. I was stupid and let my parents push me to do what I knew was the wrong thing to do."

"Well, since then he has been the male version of flighty. Cock tease. You know? Love 'em and leave 'em with not a commitment bone in his body. Now, you show back up and he is taking on the full role without batting an eye. Amazing."

"Oh, I am expecting it to fall in on him at any time. It's like waiting for the realization to hit. The penny to drop, so to speak. Then he'll know it's not what he wanted. At least this instant family, and he'll agree with me that being a weekend dad is more his style."

"I think you're wrong. I admit I wondered how he'd react but honestly, this is who he is deep down. The real Sawyer, not the one he's been playing at these last years but the real deal. He loves you. We all see it. He might be going carefully because he doesn't want to set you off. Deep down, I would lay odds on the fact that he is scared you will call it in and leave with the kids. I have to tell you, now that he knows Eli is his, you won't ever be able to go far enough. And honestly, why would you? He will raise those kids well. You need to let him in their lives for good. Yours too if you still have feelings for him. Don't push him away. You'll regret it for the rest of your life."

Piper had been putting dishes in the dishwasher. After starting the machine, she turned to Camille with a seriousness that was laced with sadness.

"I pushed and hid from Jackson for over ten years. See, if I hadn't, I wouldn't have done as well as I did in the business world but every so often, I wonder if it was worth it. I missed a lot of loving that Jackson had for me. I held every man I thought of dating or letting into my world against Jackson. He was my standard. I bet if you think back, you'll see Sawyer is your standard. And let me tell you, once you have loved a Knight, no one else will ever measure up. Don't push him away any longer. You've lost too much time already. Give yourself and your relationship a fighting chance."

"You make a good point. I'll try." Camille grabbed her purse and threw it over her arm. She hugged Piper. "Thanks for listening to me and giving me good advice. And thanks for Marla. She promises to come tomorrow to watch the children and then be there for them in the afternoon. I appreciate all the help you've given us."

"Good. You'll do the same for me sometime."

"Count on it."

After putting the sleepy children to bed, Camille went to work setting out the children's things and writing a schedule for Marla. The woman was a widow in her fifties with the sweetest, practical personality. She needed something to fill part of her time and Camille was relieved to have a woman she could feel comfortable watching the kids.

At first, Sawyer seemed hurt Camille didn't allow him to watch them until she came home but after she pointed out there were things the little ones couldn't be around, using his own words against him, he agreed.

As Cami put the final touches on the list, making sure there were enough phone numbers on the page, Sawyer looked over her shoulder. "Baby, there are still plenty of men on the ranch while you're gone. She won't need to go past my phone number but let's suppose she does, the next one is here too. Did you transfer every number off your phone list?"

"No, but don't you think it's important to have plenty of back up?"

He leaned down and kissed the top of her head.

"Absolutely."

"You think I'm overreacting."

"Nope. I think you need to do whatever makes you comfortable."

"I'm not sure anything will at first."

"Right, so do what you have to. Mrs. Dunlap will be back tomorrow to do the cooking and housekeeping. Do you remember Belinda?"

"A little. I don't think she liked me much."

"She didn't like any girl around her boys. She's gotten past that now."

"Where has she been?"

"Visiting her daughter and her sister. She'll come back with loads of gossip for the whole county." He looked at Cami in mock severity. "Don't encourage her."

"Trust me. I have been the brunt of enough gossip in my life to not want to encourage the spreading of more."

Sawyer looked as though he wanted to ask something but decided better of it. "Ready for bed, baby girl?"

"Soon. I'm going to take a quick shower and pull out my clothes for tomorrow. The more I do tonight, the easier it is in the morning. I learned that the hard way."

Sawyer opened his mouth and then closed it. She smiled. He was going to get indigestion if he kept swallowing his words, but Cami didn't intend to push. She wasn't sure she wanted to know what he was going to say. Besides, she'd kept enough of her own confidences in the last years to understand his hesitancy.

"I'll lock up and be there shortly."

"Sawyer, are you happy?"

He turned back to her. "That's an odd question, honey. I am the happiest I've been since you left."

"But that doesn't mean you're happy."

He leaned down and kissed her lips deeply. "I'm happy and getting more so every day. You?"

"Yes. It's just different isn't it? I'm happy but cautious. You know what I mean?"

"Yeah. I know. We'll get there."

"I know."

THE CHILDREN LOVED school but with everything so new, Cami's job, the town, the gossiping women, the ranch and Sawyer's daddy role, he wasn't surprised when things hit the wall on Thursday night. In some ways, literally. Cami had tried her best to make the transition as easy as possible, but the children were cranky, he had worked a long day, and Camille was so stressed she was detonating.

Walker had done well trying to keep the children entertained when it was obvious Cami was not as easygoing as earlier in the week. The kids loved Walker and vied for his attention as much as Cami's and Sawyer's. Even so, their behaviors were escalating.

Things came to a head when Eli told Lily to stop acting like a baby and Lily, in true four-year-old style, threw her spoon accurately at her brother's head, clocking him good. As he reached to stop her from throwing her milk on the crying boy, Sawyer commented on her throwing arm. Evidently, it was all Cami could handle.

"Not everything is a joke, Sawyer Knight." She jerked Lily out of her chair and put the child on her hip. The suddenness causing the preschooler to cry and reach for Sawyer who, by this time, had stood up. He started to take her and was slammed with a look so outraged he took a step back. "Don't you eff... dare." With Lily crying on her hip, Camille grabbed Eli by the hand, leading him out of the room and upstairs to the boy's great disapproval.

Sawyer let them go.

"Sorry, man. I didn't know things were so uptight." Walker sounded truly contrite.

"It's a huge transition week for them and us. Their whole routine has changed in the last month and their support system, while beefed up considerably, is still new and untried. Cami is still acting as though she has to do everything on her own as she always has and instead of asking for help, she's all but refused it."

Walker nodded. "Yeah, I think Piper called it homeostasis. Something about trying to get things back to the way they were only that won't happen in this case, so she is off-centered, trying to make a new normal."

"When did Piper get so smart?"

"Reading all those baby books. Do you know she has started a baby blog and people are reading it? I don't understand women and I'm afraid I won't ever get there. She even got Jackson to read it the other day. That man will do anything for her."

"I know the feeling." Children's distraught screeches came from upstairs. "Well, what I do understand is she needs help and like it or not, I'm giving it to her."

Walker laughed. "I'll send up some earnest prayers for you while I go over to see what Jackson is doing. I think it's about to get louder. Good thing Belinda is at bingo."

Sawyer walked towards the staircase. "Yeah, don't worry if there is a little smoke. I might need to set a small fire to clear the brush."

"Good luck with that." Walker chuckled as he grabbed his hat and truck keys before heading out the kitchen door.

Taking the steps two at a time, Sawyer listened to see which room his discontented family was occupying. It only took two seconds to home in on Eli's response to his overstressed mother.

"I want my daddy. He's nice. He loves me."

Taking a deep breath, Sawyer entered the lion's den, also known as the children's room. He really needed to make this room more kid friendly. He mentally added it to the ever-growing list of things to do outside of the ranch's equestrian business, which was his primary work responsibility. Each brother had his own aspect of the business. His was horses. Breeding was over for this year and he was busy setting things up for winter. And now, settling his family.

"Hey, what's all the ruckus about up here? I thought there was a stampede of wild mustangs trying to get out, with all this caterwauling."

Eli and Lily immediately ran to him and he caught them, swinging each up in an arm.

"Sawyer, you are undermining me and that isn't what good parents do."

He turned to look hard at Camille. She'd been crying, and that was not going to work for him. "I'm doing what a good partner and parent would do, helping."

"I have this under control," Camille said through gritted teeth.

"No, baby girl, you do not have this under control. You have some ill-conceived notion you don't have support. That you still must do everything alone and I'm here to tell you, that isn't how we roll. I have always had your back and more now than ever before."

"They are my responsibility, not yours."

"And that's where you're wrong. The moment they called me daddy, these little screamers became my primary responsibility. Don't shut me out because then I'll have to break down the door. Don't make me have to remind you my preferred method of getting through to you."

"You wouldn't dare."

"Sweetheart, you are way past having earned it, but more than that, you are too tightly strung and likely need it. You'd agree if you allowed yourself to open up a little. We'll work on that a little later on tonight." He jiggled the two squirming children in his arms. "Right now, we have two tired children to bathe and put to bed."

Sawyer wasn't sure if he was making the best choice as far as raising children was concerned but it felt right and he knew, for their relationship, it was right. He nodded in the dresser's direction that held the children's clothing.

"Get me some sleepers and then climb in the shower. I'll finish here."

Cami opened her mouth again. "Now, baby girl. Let me take care of you."

She nodded and pulled out nightclothes as he took two restless munchkins to the hall bathroom. After bathing and explaining how their behavior was unacceptable, Sawyer put them to bed, noticing how quickly they snuggled in under the comforter.

"Daddy, can you make Mama feel better too?" He reached to kiss the top of his boy's head.

"I'm going to do my best, son."

Chapter 8

Cami stepped out of the shower. The hot spray felt good on her aching muscles and her sore head. Sawyer was right. Why was she fighting him so much when he wanted to take part of the load? He couldn't help her in her nursing job any more than she could breed world class equestrian champions, but they could share the rest, the parenting. Some days he'd do more than she did and some days it would be her turn but it would balance. It would take one more bit of stress off her back.

The trouble was it was hard to relinquish any of her control. It sounded good on paper but in reality, she had held tight to the reins so nothing and no one could stand in the way of her responsibilities to her children and reaching her personal goals toward independence, but sometimes it was exhausting. Correction, all the time. It should be easier because she didn't have to pick them up or have them delivered to a daycare that she then must reverse the process after work. She didn't have to cook dinner unless she wanted to because Belinda did that as well as clean house. And yet, by evening, she was completely drained.

She acknowledged it was the newness of everything and even the people, some of whom she knew, were different-at least they treated her differently. They treated her as though she were deceiving them about why she left, the time she was away, and why she came back. As though they had every right to demand full disclosure. She didn't tell much, and she had no female to confide in besides Piper but the rumor mill was working hard, overtime she imagined, dreaming up scenarios about her life.

Cami wanted to tell Sawyer about her fears as to the gossip, etc., but she had given him so much to make room for on his already full plate, she didn't dare make it even more difficult. She needed to be left to live her life the way she saw fit, like anyone else. Hadn't she earned that right? Why did people have to make judgements about others? And if one more person made a speculation about the last name she now had, well, she couldn't be held responsible for her actions. In her fantasy world, anyway. Camille sighed.

Hanging the towel back on the rack, she brushed her teeth and hair before going to the dresser she shared with Sawyer. She pulled out a tee shirt from his drawer, hoping the comfort it gave her to wear it would help her sleep. She began to pull it over her head when the shirt was taken from her hands.

"The kids were so tired, they barely made it into bed before they were sleeping." His deep, steady voice soothed her as he kissed her neck.

"I'm sorry you had to do that and sorry about the shirt. It was presumptuous." He was the most handsome man she had ever known and to think he still had eyes for her was almost too unbelievable for words. She was tempted, at least once a day, to pinch herself. He patted her backside suggestively.

He tossed the shirt on the dresser and turned her to stand fully in front of the mirror on top. He held her tight to his body, his outdoorsman scent surrounding her. He'd showered when he came in tonight so the clean woodsy aroma of his body wash added to his spicy deodorant and his natural male essence almost made her weak in the knees. It was the aroma of safety. Protection. Love.

"You can wear it later if you need it. You can always wear my things. I love seeing you in them. It calms my possessive heart. But we have some things to discuss, beautiful. And the first thing—his take charge voice and manner thrilled her—is you never say you're sorry I had to take care of the children. We share that responsibility completely." She looked down. His fingertip tapped under her chin, bringing her head back up. "Say 'yes, Sawyer.'"

"Are you sure?" Their eyes met in the mirror.

"What did I just say?" His eyes never wavered from hers. "How do you answer me?"

"Yes, Sawyer." Her nipples hardened further, almost painfully.

"Good girl." He kissed the top of her head and drew her back against his front. "Now, tell me why you're so stressed."

She turned and spoke into his chest. "It's just getting a routine down."

"And what else?"

"Nothing." She couldn't tell him about how hard some people were making it for her. Nor could she look him in the eye when she was untruthful. She never had been able to do that. Sawyer could look into her very soul, always could. Or maybe it had just been her guilt, which she carried around for every little infraction like a shameful banner of honor. But that wouldn't happen now. She was stronger.

"What have I always said about keeping the truth from me?"

"I'm not. Honest." She leaned into his t-shirt covered chest. He couldn't really know.

"Is that your last answer, baby girl?"

"Yes, because it's the truth."

Her heart was beating faster, she knew it, and her head was beginning to pound as it always did when she lied to him. On top of her headache, it was definitely painful. She wasn't lying, she told herself, it really wasn't anything. Normal stuff. Nothing out of the ordinary.

"I'm glad you have decided to be naughty, baby, because I've wanted to heat this bottom up for several weeks. From the first night you appeared at Piper and Jackson's house, actually." Camille attempted to step back but only her feet moved. Sawyer had her held tight to him. "Let's get you into position."

"No, you can't possibly believe that I'll allow you to spank me like you used to, Sawyer. I'm an adult. I have children."

"No? Are you telling your daddy, no?"

Camille heard the demanding words and her core clenched, her belly flexed, her mouth went dry. "Yes. I am telling you no way." Her voice sounded like sandpaper.

"I've missed your sass, honey. And to remind you of the lay of the land these days, those are our children, baby. The courts have signed off, remember? Legally, and practically, and in my heart, those are just as much my children as yours." He kissed her. "And so is their mother."

Picking her up and sitting on the edge of the bed, he had her over his knee way too fast. He took some time to brush her hair out of the way and rub circles on her back before he moved down to pat her bare bottom. Camille could feel the chill raise bumps on her skin and the shiver that came with it uncontrolled.

"We have some things to discuss, sweetheart. This is as good a place to do it as any."

"Sawyer," she rasped, "the children."

"Are asleep, did I not tell you that? The walls and doors are heavy. And before you bring up Walker or Belinda, they won't be back for a while. And even if they were, Belinda's bedroom is off the kitchen and Walker has moved downstairs so he doesn't wake the kids up when he gets in the shower at five in the morning."

"Sawyer, please," Camille begged him to change his mind although her contrary body was aching for him to continue.

"As I was saying, we're going to talk about a few things. The first is when you found out you were pregnant why didn't you call me?"

"I told you I didn't think he was yours. I thought since we hadn't had sex in two months, it was likely to be Aiden's. Besides, my parents wanted me to leave town before anyone could figure it out. And I thought you wouldn't want me." His hand landed on her bottom, sizzling it good. "Please, Sawyer, that hurts."

"Then I haven't lost my touch. Now, why didn't you believe in me and my love?" When Camille was silent, he rained down four more loud, solid smacks to her butt.

"Try again, Cami."

"I thought you couldn't love me because I was unlovable. I was your plaything but everything we had planned wouldn't mean anything because another man had touched me. Gotten me pregnant when I was meant to have your babies."

The tears fell and rather than him landing more painful thought changers, as he used to call them, he patted her bottom in a light drumming rhythm. Not quite painful but warming and oddly comforting. As he increased the strength of those swats ever so slightly, she could feel her libido dancing to the beat of his hand. Her tears slowed.

"I. Have. Always. Loved. You," he said, punctuating every word with a swat. "I. Will. Always. Love. You." More swats. "You hurt me and us, when you decided your course of action, on your own."

His swats were back to four swift stinging strikes. She could feel her breaths coming faster.

"My mother said you wouldn't want used goods."

"Well she lied or more like she had no idea what I would think or want. You, however, were intimately aware of how I thought. That's what hurts."

Camille cried in earnest then. She had wasted all this time and she could have been happy. She cried for the loss of time, for the times she was alone and missed him. For the time she cheated all of them. But she couldn't be sorry for Lily.

"I'm sorry. I ruined everything but I can't imagine my life without Lily and she came about because of that monster."

"No, you didn't ruin everything, because you're here now, with me, where you belong. And I love that baby girl in the other room who is so much like her sassy mama. But you do have some penance." He rubbed her back again in a circular motion before continuing. "The second issue is why didn't you call me when that jackass left you?" He couldn't call him her husband.

He didn't agree he was. "When you found out Eli was my son? Or even when he left you for another woman and didn't offer to send you or Eli home. Why did you stay away for so long? You knew I would come and get you."

"Actually, I didn't. I still thought you wouldn't want him. I was already convinced you didn't want me." His hand scorched her bottom.

"Why are you spanking me when I'm being honest?" she cried out.

"Because that is faulty thinking, woman. I love you. I always have. I'll keep reminding you until the cows come home and beyond. You need to change the way you see me, us."

"How can you say that after all I've done? After all, I've kept from you?"

"Because it's the truth, baby. Lord help me, I love you to the very core of my being."

"But I don't deserve it." Her tears returned.

"None of that, my girl. You deserve love. We deserve this new chance. We need to get rid of this leftover guilt."

His hand landed heavily. The tempo was fast, and the burn was growing hotter with every swat. Her breathing was rough and her lady bits were throbbing. On and on he pounded while she resisted the emotional release she knew he thought she should have and that she was afraid to indulge in.

Finally, she heard his voice crack when he said, "Camille, I have loved you forever and I will love you til the end of time. Please give me a chance to prove to you I can be the man you need, the one you want. The one you won't ever leave."

That did it. Her flood gates opened. She needed him so much, had wanted to be in his arms for so long, how could she deny a man who obviously loved her as much as she loved him? She didn't deserve him but she wanted to. Sometime during her release, she found herself on the bed, wrapped in his arms. He had stripped off his shirt so he could hold her tight against his warm flesh.

Finally, she had slowed the tears enough to hear his words of comfort. How did such a wonderful man exist after she had left him? Yes, things were awkward. Different. Strange at times. She had spent most of her teen years here, on this ranch, in this house and now she was a visitor, her life then, a distant memory. And yet, somehow, she was home. More than her parents' house, here was where she felt she belonged. She'd make it hers again.

She wasn't the person she had been when she left. None of them were but she could give them a chance, like he asked. Sawyer was her past but more importantly, he was her future. She was lied to by people that she trusted then but now, she had her eyes wide open and she was staring at Sawyer.

"Better? Is the guilt all gone?"

"Almost."

"What's left? I don't have the heart to spank you any more tonight, baby. Can't you just tell me?"

She nodded. She could tell him. "People are saying harsh things about me being here with you. They say so many things but one of the hardest to hear is that you took me back out of pity because I tricked you into thinking Eli was yours."

"Fuck. Have they seen that boy? Do they know me? The only important thing here is this, do you think that?"

She stuttered out a depreciative laugh. "Not any longer."

He released a guttural sound. "You thought that even after I said how much he looked like me? How I refuse to let you take him from me? I should spank you again."

"No! Wait, you said you couldn't do that again tonight."

"Might have changed my mind."

"Sawyer, think. I didn't know you, not after the separation. I even thought you were married to Piper for an hour or so." Then she laughed. It felt good.

"Damn woman, you tell yourself all kinds of things that make me want to spank your ass." He kissed her sternly.

She reached to rub her assaulted bottom. "I can't handle any more of your method of fixing things, Sawyer." He grinned. "And I didn't believe it until I heard it then I have to admit, I did wonder for a little, but I don't believe it. I believe you love me. I feel better. The stress is much less, the guilt and worry isn't weighing me down now. I can handle the gossip. Do you know how hard your hand is? You never spanked me that hard before."

"I think I did when you jumped from the loft to get away from me. Remember? When you didn't want to go home after your eighteenth birthday. Tonight, I just had a lot to cover in a short amount of time."

"Hmm. If you would have let me stay, we wouldn't have been in this predicament in the first place."

"Ah, so it's my fault?"

"In a manner of speaking, yes." She cuddled in as close as she could get. "Daddy?"

"I love that."

"What?"

"When you call me daddy. I love it. Which brings me to a daddy issue. You swore at me downstairs tonight." His tone was all Daddy-dom and Camille gushed.

"I didn't. I stopped from saying the f-bomb because of the kids."

"But you were saying it on the inside."

She giggled. "I say a lot of things inside that you never know about, but that isn't the same thing."

"Sweetheart, it is in my book." He landed a loud fleshy slap on her butt. "Don't do it again. Daddies do not like their little girls swearing. Ever."

"You did."

"I'll have to learn to curb the impulse now I have little ones to be the example for."

"Hmm, what about big girls?"

"I'll take it under advisement." His hand slid up the slender column of her neck and tangled into her silky hair, fisting it. Camille whimpered from the arousal that one act released.

"Now, Daddy is going to do what he wants with his girl and she's going to take it."

"It's been so long."

"For me too. I took out all sorts of women for a while, tried to take them to bed, but could never feel for them anything close to what I feel for you. Don't get me wrong, I had plenty of desperate sex to scratch an itch, but nothing serious. I was the town challenge for women but I couldn't be unfaithful to you, although you will hear plenty of rumors to the contrary."

"Other than both times he forced himself on me, I didn't have sex with Aiden. He liked the fight and so he looked for other women who would give him that, I guess. When he found out Eli wasn't his that was the legal end. I rarely saw him until the DNA returned. He took me the night he was leaving for good. Anyway, I say that to announce that I don't know how good I will be."

"Cami, you have always been perfect for me."

His lips came crashing to meet hers. Punishing, going deeper, drawing out her sweetness, struggling with her tenaciousness. His tongue battled its way into her mouth and danced with hers. His lips found her cheeks, her neck, the tender flesh behind her ear, raising goosebumps again, as her body temperature rose in direct correlation to his fiery touch.

The way he kissed horizontal lines on her belly, she knew he'd found her stretch marks from bearing two children without him. He hesitated and her mind felt those pauses longer than they were but then she felt his tongue trace the deepest scars. His kisses were his acceptance of their existence and the circumstances surrounding them. Her heart swelled from the kindness of this man. He had accepted her when she expected rejection. Loved her when she'd expected hatred. She had no option but to trust him completely. What a relief to her soul.

Her hand slipped down, hurriedly trying to unbuckle his belt, unbutton his pants, and slide her hand inside. He let her explore. She was kissing his chest, his nipples, sucking, licking before she returned her attention to his pants. Without a word, Sawyer helped her and finished undressing, kicking the clothing out of his way before sliding down to the apex of her thighs. Her trimmed mons was soon wet from his tongue that seemed to be everywhere at once.

"Mmm. When did you do this?" he brushed her mons with his breath.

She dragged her mind, drunk on arousal, to think on his question. "This? Trim? Yesterday." She felt his lips form a smile. "You remembered."

One hand was flicking her clit in between circling and teasing. His other hand was holding her folds open to his further exploration and even that was sexy as hell. She was firing her rockets before he had been there long. Her orgasm brought on a rainbow of colors that danced behind her eyes, nearly overcoming her. His scent was surrounding her, the air was thin and heady, thick and overwhelming at the same time. Her muscles, even as she came back to herself were flexing, twinging. Finally, she took a cleansing breath and smiled.

Sawyer watched his girl in gentle amazement as she climaxed for him. It was the first time in six years and it was the most incredible sight. It seemed like the first time. She was swept away and lost in the feelings of release. He did that for her. His cock was rock hard. His ball sack was tight, putting pressure on its contents and there was a distinct pull in his groin. He needed to come in the worst way but he needed to see her ignite once more. If he waited, she wouldn't go again for a while, but if he came at her again now, right after the first time, she'd shoot off multiple times before she was too sensitive to go any more. Then he'd take his pleasure.

They had never climaxed together except when he manipulated her clit just right. He remembered everything about making love to her. He remembered her panting breaths right before she climaxed. Her excited squeals when he'd tease her into making love. Her whines and whimpers when her orgasm had been held off for longer than she thought she could handle. And her insatiable appetite for more.

Climbing over her again, he grabbed her wrists in one hand, pinning them above her head, while settling between her slick legs, his sweaty body taking up position over hers. He leaned down to excite her tits again before leaving them reluctantly for her clit. She loved being tied down, pinned, taken, but he wondered if she'd ever be comfortable with total bondage again after being violated by the man he would cheerfully kill, not once but twice.

Letting his thirst for vengeance go for now, Sawyer slid into her waiting sheath as he brought her off again. She cried out but in ecstasy, not terror. He leaned down to kiss her lips before releasing her hands.

"Hold the headboard, sweetheart. It's time for this cowboy to ride."

His voice was raspy and rough, full of the emotions racing through him. He loved that in the throes of passion, she obeyed without question. If he could get more of that outside the bedroom... But sassy was good too. He took her slowly at first. With his hands now on her hips, he slid inside, waited, pulled out. When she gave her impatient sounds, he knew she was fine and plunged into paradise.

In and out in the age-old mating rhythm, Sawyer was lost in the feeling, relishing the clenching of her inner muscles massaging his cock. His release was like a pressurized chemical reaction, he was lightheaded. He fell to the bed beside Cami and realized, when he reached to remove the condom, that he hadn't worn any.

His breathing normalized as he contemplated how he would handle this. Fuck, how was she going to react to him losing control so much he forgot to glove up? He needed to get it out of the way now, while she was still mellow. He wanted complete honesty from her and he would give her nothing less. He leaned into Cami and whispered in her ear.

"Cami, I'm so sorry baby, I forgot a condom." He waited for the fall out but there wasn't any.

She simply turned with a bemused look on her face and said, "Mmm hmm."

She then rolled over, snuggled her butt into his crotch, and promptly fell asleep. It was late. What was done was done. He'd talk to her tomorrow. He hoped his greatest worry didn't come to pass. No use losing sleep over it if she wasn't. But he did. It was another hour before he slipped into his own blissful slumber.

The next morning, when he tried to tell Camille he had taken her without protection, she said, "I heard you last night. I can't fix that now and neither can you. We'll be more careful next time."

He must have mellowed her a lot last night because most women would have lost their composure and yelled down the house. Not Cami, she almost seemed to ignore it. Maybe she was on birth control. He'd have to remember to ask tonight. She wasn't the only one ignoring things, or rather people. Belinda was having an obvious issue with Camille and he intended to get to the bottom of it after everyone else had left the house.

Sawyer stood in the doorway of the barn as he watched Camille and the kids drive away. He finished his chore and headed back to the kitchen to pour another cup of coffee. Walker, having started work earlier so he could leave at four for Josie's Austin apartment, saw the look on his brother's face.

Grabbing his snack and coffee, he left Sawyer and Belinda in the house alone.

Sawyer had suggested to his brother that morning that Josie come to the ranch for the weekend, but Walker said Josie wasn't ready for all of them at one time yet. Sawyer pointed out she handled it fine before, but he wouldn't change his mind. Well, that was fine with him. Sawyer had enough on his plate right now and not having to make room for more was a relief.

He started by asking about Belinda's bingo night. He apologized for not having asked about her vacation earlier in the month. Belinda continued to clean the kitchen as they talked, seeming to want a distance between them. Good call. After going through the events of her time off, watching as the kitchen was cleaned and dinner things laid out, he decided it was time he probed further.

"Belinda, I noticed you were having a hard morning. Is there anything that I can do? Do you still enjoy working here? Are the kids too much for you? I had hoped that having Marla here while Lily was home in the afternoons would relieve you of any burden in that regard."

Sawyer knew he could have been touchier about people's reaction to Camille, especially since he had overheard some nastiness, but this was his home and now Cami and the children's. He wouldn't have discord here. Belinda could be having a bad day, end of story. He wanted to give her the benefit of the doubt, be fair, but the way she didn't look him in the eye, told him she might not deserve it.

"I wasn't going to say anything, but since you brought it up, I'll be honest with you." Belinda looked him in the eye, her gaze never wavering. "I think you might have made a grave error in judgement."

"Not unheard of, so what does it concern?" He liked Belinda. She'd been with them for a few years and he hoped they could see their way through this, but his expectations were not high.

"That Hendrix woman. She has snowed you. Everyone knows it. Bringing kids she says are yours. Acting as though she is a victim. I can tell you there are a lot of things you don't know."

Taking a moment to cool his temper and settle his thoughts, Sawyer indicated the chair across from him and took a drink of coffee.

"I know what I know, but why don't you tell me what you believe to be true."

"Well," the woman hesitated before continuing. "She left the kid's father and came home because he kicked her out, for one. Her husband was a good man, making a good living." When there was no response from Sawyer, she continued, "There's talk of extra-marital affairs. Even her mother says she is a woman of loose morals."

"I see." Sawyer was formulating his response when Belinda went on. "And that woman is using you to find a place for her and another man's children. Even her own mother won't take them in because of who she is. She left you all those years ago because she thought she had found a bigger fish."

"And you are positive of this information? Have proof?"

"I don't need it. It's she that has the proof of it but what mother would say such things about her child if it weren't true?"

"I am the father listed on those children's birth certificates. I have DNA paperwork, not that it would matter. Camille, Eli, named after me, and Lily, named after her mother, are my family. I will defend them to the ends of the earth against all takers." He deliberately kept control, but it was using all his emotional efforts.

She didn't seem convinced, but it was obviously information she didn't have before now. Irrationally, the woman continued, "Well, sir, you should know that I defended you and Walker. Plenty of the group said you were naïve and didn't know about love. You were chasing after rainbows, the three of you, keeping one woman in your heart when there are so many ready to give any of you what you need. There are plenty of women who would do right by you, Sawyer. Not used, devious, immoral women, but good ones. You could have your pick."

"Yes, like your daughter for one."

"For one, yes. You could do worse."

"I'm sure I would be doing worse if I left Camille and the kids because I love her. You weren't around when we were growing up on this ranch but the living wasn't easy. I was ten when my mother died. My father was a good man but then he got lonely. Found that alcohol could alleviate that loneliness. Then he wasn't as good a man any longer. We boys spent plenty of nights in the barn. Then, Camille walked into my life, and I never looked back."

He took a drink of his coffee and looked Belinda in the eye.

"I've loved her since she came with a group of sixth graders to ride. I don't know if you understand what that means, seeing as you have been divorced twice. With that type of history, I imagine it's easy for you to believe falling out of love isn't difficult since you've done it at least twice."

"That's not true." The aggressive response signaled he'd hit a nerve. Good.

"Assumptions are painful things, aren't they?"

"Her mother said—"

"Guilt. Her mother is speaking out of guilt. See, there's a whole lot of reality that's been left out of the telling of your story that you need to hear. First, the man Camille's mother forced her to marry, raped her. She didn't go with him willingly; she was given no choice."

"What?"

The kitchen door slammed. Walker and Cami were standing in the mud room staring at Sawyer and Belinda. They appeared frozen in place, obviously having heard some of their conversation. How much was only a guess at this juncture? Sawyer looked into Camille's eyes, questioning why she was there but she didn't respond. He smiled tenderly. She didn't indicate she'd even seen him.

Walker tried to turn her around, but she refused his direction. Sawyer caught Walker's eye, passing a message between the two of them. Hell, they'd heard enough, and he needed her out of the room. He wasn't done with their housekeeper and Camille didn't need to listen to them. Tipping his head and moving his eyes in the direction of upstairs, he hoped his brother read him clearly.

Walker's low voice, full of gravel and dominance, could be heard but not the words he used. Cami looked at Sawyer then. He nodded to encourage her to do whatever Walker was instructing her. She raced through the kitchen and soon the padding from her sneakers on wooden steps were heard, followed by Walker's heavy thudding boots.

"Like I started to say, I'm going to tell you the real story."

By the end, Belinda was crying in horror of the truth. "That poor child. Why would her mother say and do those things? It isn't natural. I have to apologize to her and set the rest of them straight."

"No, that's my job. You can apologize later. I'll handle my family's information. It isn't your information to share, but I would encourage you not to join in the nastiness." Sawyer spoke in his boss voice. A tone that exuded a no-nonsense dominance leaving her no doubt as to the seriousness of this occurrence.

"Yes, sir."

"Gossip is destructive and spreading it without checking your facts with the source you are talking about will get you fired without a reference you would otherwise have earned. I'm hopeful we won't have to deal with it again." Belinda nodded. "And our personal lives are ours. No one will dictate to us who we love and certainly not for how long. Do we have an understanding?"

"Yes, sir. We do. And please tell Miss Hendrix, I'm sorry."

"Knight. She and the children have the last name of Knight. Another thing you obviously didn't know."

"Yes, sir."

Sawyer left the woman to figure out how to get past her grave errors in believing gossip. His baby girl was upstairs instead of at work for some reason. She had overheard some of the conversation he had hoped she would never hear. He could only imagine what was going through her mind right now. As he topped the stairs, he could hear muffled crying. Walker was sitting outside Sawyer and Cami's bedroom, keeping watch.

"Did ya fire her?" Walker asked as he stood.

"Belinda? Nope. We will if it ever happens again though. I think I've avoided it happening again for any of us."

Walker nodded and tipped his head in the direction of the door. "She's been in there, crying, since we came up. Door's locked."

Sawyer sighed loudly. "Why is she home, anyway?"

"Said there was an incident at the school. Said she couldn't deal with the snide remarks today. Allowed by the superintendent, no less. Need me to set old Watkins straight? I've about had it with a lot of things. I could use a little stress relief."

Sawyer ran his hands over his shaved face. "I'll handle him later. Looks like I won't be working much today. Think you could cover for me this morning? Tell my guys not to look for me to get back? I'll cover for you this afternoon if you want to leave sooner for Austin."

"You don't have to do that. I'll always have your back. Hey, Sawyer, I never told you how happy I am for you and Camille. I hope Josie and I can get there too."

Sawyer looked at Walker hard. "You love her?"

"I do."

"Whatever you need, you know you only have to ask."

"Thanks. Jackson said the same thing last night. Now, you'd better open the door and take care of your girl in there." Walker slapped his brother on the back and headed toward the stairs.

Sawyer noticed the abject crying had now stopped. That was a good thing, right? "Cami, let me in, baby."

There was shuffling inside but no movement near the door. "Cami."

He knew the exact tone that would send chills up her spine; he'd seen her reaction plenty of times to be confident. Maybe she thought he believed the garbage Belinda had said this morning. If that were true, he'd address that later. He wasn't sure she'd heard much if anything. He wanted to hold her, reassure her and ask her to marry him. Then he could move on to find out just how heavy he needed to come down on the asinine superintendent, only then could he fix any errant thinking. The communities' and his girl's.

"Camille Constance Knight, if you have any thoughts of self-preservation, you will open this door yourself."

She didn't respond except to sniffle a little louder. He couldn't break down the door for several reasons, but the biggest one being its material: thick, solid wood. The hinges were heavy, the whole damn house was built like Fort Knox. It's just how his great-grandparents had built it. To last. He thought about getting the screwdriver out but really, this was a test for both of them. One he intended to pass.

"Camilly Piccadilly, open the door for Daddy. I know you've had a crap day, mine hasn't started the best either, but we can talk it through and then take care of things. I love you, baby, open the door."

Movement, good, he was getting through to her. Yep, she was definitely walking to the door. "Go away."

Not good. He'd have to strengthen his deliverance. "Camille, games are over. If you expect to get out of this little incident with your butt intact, I suggest very strongly that you open this door. I know you're upset, but I can't listen to what happened or hold you with a locked block of wood between us."

She spoke from the other side of the barrier. "Ironic, isn't it? The one thing I thought coming home would do is give me a sense of peace, belonging. Man, did I misread things."

"Yep, not having this conversation with you on the other side of the door. You can stand in there, complaining, but you will have to come out for the children. For dinner. And when you do, I'll be here. I won't say your spanking won't grow in correlation to your naughtiness, but I can wait you out. Question is, can you afford to make me? And do you want to wait until the kids get home, so they see you get your butt heated a fiery red? Something to think about."

The sniffling had stopped. It sounded as though she had moved away from the door. He heard the slight creak of the bed. Yeah, it might be a long wait and now, while he still wanted to reassure her, he wanted to paddle that obstinate bottom just as much. He slid down the wall to sit on the floor and wait her out.

While he did, he planned his next steps.

Chapter 9

What was she doing? Sawyer meant every word he said about loving her, taking care of her and taking her in hand. Her sex clenched at the thought of Sawyer in any capacity but owning her topped the list. It might not be for everyone, but it was for her. She loved him so much it hurt. Really, physically hurt. Her stomach tightened and tumbled in anticipation of him. Her brain seized with the mere thought of him, of being his.

And her core? Those romance novels had no idea the strength of the message a woman's core sent when the man she was meant to be with was available to her. Nor did they adequately describe the gut-wrenching pain that physically invaded her system when he wasn't available.

This all-consuming need was more than desire, beyond want, it was survival. Her whole being demanded his presence to fill the poverty of her soul that existed without him. And now she had him. Trying to do the right thing for everyone else had proven to be the exact wrong thing. Aiden had never wanted to marry her once he found out she wasn't who he thought she was. Not her fault but still, if she had believed that Sawyer was stronger than her parents and Aiden, she'd have been happy all these years. She didn't regret her Lily. Never. But she regretted she wasn't conceived in a loving relationship.

She would've been happy to do what was necessary to get Sawyer to understand back then. Now she knew he would have been able to weather that storm negating her need to survive all the other squalls that came afterwards. Because she was manipulated too easily by her parents, she had missed carefree nights wishing on shooting stars with Sawyer as they waited for their child. No more youthful endeavors like skinny-dipping. No making love in the barn or even experiencing romantic love since leaving Sawyer. No kisses at dawn. She gave it all up for her parent's dignity and later to raise her children. And she'd been lonely.

Camille had worked hard to make a living and survive. No one had the right to judge her on the choices she had made. She'd done what she could. No man or woman had the right to say otherwise unless they had lived her life, and she wasn't going to allow them to trash her sacrifices. Conflict was something she had run from most of her life, preferring to stand in the shadows, out of the limelight of those people and events around her. This time was different. It had to be different. She loved Sawyer and refused to give him and this life up without a damn good fight.

Camille knew what she had to do. Grabbing her jacket, purse, and keys, Cami yanked the door open and walked into the hard, fragrant maleness of her man.

"Camille, honey, where are you going?"

"I need to do something."

"What exactly? Because I don't mind telling you, while this rough, well used look you're sporting makes me stiff, you might not want the rest of the world to think you were ridden hard and put away wet."

"I should have known my equestrian expert would use that analogy. I'm going to have it out with Mr. Watkins." She pushed him to give herself an exit.

"No, that isn't the way we're going to do it."

"No? Did you just tell me no?"

His grin was easy and full of his amusement. "I think that's my line, sweetheart."

"I shouldn't need to remind you that I have taken care of myself since I left here. That I have had two babies I took care of alone."

His tone and facial expression hardened in seriousness. "And I shouldn't have to remind you it isn't my fault you did that."

Her anger was gone but her righteous indignation flag was flying high. "I know you would have been there with me if you'd known. That is definitely on me and my ignorance. But I earned a degree and supported my babies alone. I'm not used to anyone standing up for me nor am I sure I can handle it. I've worked hard for where I am, and I'll be damned if that old wrinkle face is going to ask me about my personal life."

He tried to pull her into his arms, but she wasn't going to have it. He'd take all her firepower and redistribute it, but she needed it to keep her momentum going. She pushed him away.

"Camille." She almost imploded with the power of that one word spoken by the man who loved her, respected her... expected her compliance.

"I'm sorry. I have to do this." Camille looked at Sawyer, the man she had loved since she was twelve and they were still children. "Please?" she begged.

"Not this way."

"Yes, dammit. This way." She was too irritated to notice he had stepped into her space effectively eliminating any advance she had made. He'd begun to walk her back into the room. By the time she did realize his movements, it was all but too late. "No, Sawyer."

"Yes. Baby girl, your 'yeses' and 'noes' are in the wrong places. Let me untangle them for you."

She had been in this position before, more times than she cared to count, but he hadn't placed her in it this quickly very often. "Please, Sawyer."

"I know you recognize what room we are in, what position you hold in this room."

"I don't think I earned this."

"No? Well, I see it differently. You told me no when I said you were going to have to handle things differently." His hand fell hard, the swats coming faster than she could comprehend. He stopped and rubbed her bottom. "You're upset but not sharing what happened. You're pushing me away again. Is that allowed?"

Camille knew it wasn't. Not because she wasn't entitled to her own thoughts, but it hurt their relationship. Sawyer's expectations on togetherness included openness and sharing. They had been intricate parts of a healthy relationship from the beginning and hadn't changed since she first accepted a date with him. He said he'd officially claimed her that night and there was no going back. He never had. Regardless of the life she had been pushed to live, in reality, neither had she. This man was what she needed to breathe.

"No, Daddy."

"That's my girl. Daddy has a little more to get through here while you explain what really happened at school. I imagine it happened as you arrived because you weren't gone long enough for it to be any later." He spoke as though he were having a leisurely conversation, but his swats had resumed.

"Camille, the attorney got our birth certificates yesterday. I got a text message while I was waiting for you to open a door that shouldn't have been locked against me."

She knew this Sawyer. He was in control. She swung her free hand up to cover her bottom instinctively. Sawyer grabbed her unencumbered hand and tugged her tighter to his body, accomplishing three very important things. He pinned her inside arm with no hope of getting loose. He pressed his hard cock against her belly. His dominance, and the protection she felt as a result left her wet. She felt the twinge and fluid release much like when she heard her baby cry and her milk flowed. Her sex did the same. She whined.

"I'm sorry I didn't let you in, but I was upset." He stopped then, resuming rubbing her back.

"I know, honey, but that's when you should let me in automatically and I don't mean just in the room."

He was right, damn him. "I know. I'm trying."

"And I'm helping you. See how this works?" There was a smile in his words. The smacks began again. Hard, measured swats that stung, burned, sank deep into her soul, and began to heal her brokenness. "I love you, Camille. Always have and always will. Marry me."

"I love you... wait... what did you say?" Did he ask her to marry him? Really ask her? She'd dreamed of this day. As a teen, she had fallen into his plans for their life. There was never a proposal, just an assumption. She had created the scene over and over but never saw it come to fruition and never while over his lap!

"You need more? Lying to your daddy while you are in this very vulnerable position is never a good idea, little girl." His words were full of yearning, and the gravel in his tone was incredibly sexy.

"But you can't ask me that while you are pounding my ass, Sawyer!"

"No?"

He really had to consider her words. This man was so used to control he didn't know when he didn't have it. She needed to show him. She softened her tone.

"No, Sawyer, you can't. You can't make me say yes."

"Oh, little girl, you are so wrong, because I can get you to do whatever I want. But you're right in that I don't want to make you say yes. I want it to be a real answer to a real question. Up, baby."

He helped her straighten, settled her on the bed next to him then pushed her to her back. His mouth came down, his lips landed on hers, hungry and impatient. The man was no slacker when it came to kissing. She'd often wondered if he'd practiced kissing, like girls did, in a mirror or something. Regardless of whether it was a natural ability, or a practiced skill, he was too hot to ignore. When he lifted his head, propping himself above her she followed, pulling him back down for more.

"Don't get used to this, little girl. Daddy likes to be in charge but sometimes, it's hot to know you want me at least as much as I want you. How about you help Daddy undress and you can go for a ride this morning? I'll take over tonight."

"Yes please," came her teasing answer as she quickly eliminated his clothing and hers. Sawyer massaged her breasts before moving on to her bottom still warm from his spanking. Touching and kissing his work-honed body excited her and to have free range over him as he reciprocated took all other thought.

Sliding her hands down his chest, over his chiseled belly and down to his cock, flanked by neatly trimmed, soft but wiry hair, she ran her fingers lightly over his manhood. He kissed her as she grabbed his member. Her teasing laugh seemed to harden him more. Camille slid down between his thighs and licked the precum from the purple-headed stalk. Kissing, licking, sucking his cock, making noises of pure enjoyment was heady.

She smiled when he tangled his fingers in her hair. Her man couldn't do as he often demanded of her: just lie there and accept the loving. He had to take some control. He held her steady as he began pumping into her mouth. Giving in to his control released more liquid arousal. She could feel it slipping onto her thighs.

Untangling his hands from her hair, he pulled her up towards his lips as she kissed his torso on her way back up to his face.

"My turn, now," he whispered in a strangled harsh voice.

"Not fair, you stole some of my time."

"Never said I was fair. It's Daddy's turn. Now climb on like a good girl."

"I still get to ride?" she asked eagerly as she positioned herself just right to mount him. "What kind are you?"

"What kind?"

"What kind of horse?"

His deep chuckle made her tummy flip. "You're riding the cowboy, baby. They are so much more inventive."

He brought her down onto his cock, fully seating her over him. Claiming her, showing her he not only took care of his woman, but he also took her. He held her in one position while he pumped her for a while and then allowed her to ride him. As she began to tingle from the friction of the pounding of her clit on every meeting of their pelvises, he demanded something he'd never said to her before.

"Touch yourself, Camille. Bring yourself off."

"What? I can't do that. It's embarrassing."

"Can you argue with Daddy?"

"No, but I can argue with my boyfriend."

"Fiancé," he growled. "But when we're in here, you don't talk back. Daddy rules this room, not his little girl."

"Fuck that."

"I'm trying to," he said as he slowed his movements. He released her hips and brought her down, chest to chest. The next thing she felt and heard was an explosion on her butt, then another one. Over and over she felt the sharp slaps on her backside as he continued to pump slowly.

"Please, it hurts."

"Would you like another chance to do as I said?"

Camille didn't know how she'd touch herself in front of him but somehow, she would. She nodded. "Yes. I can try."

He nodded and helped her sit up straight on his staff then watched as she tentatively inched towards her clit. Two thigh slaps made her inch faster. *Don't think about it, just do it.* She touched herself and it felt forbidden. That gave it more power, and she was soon rubbing and circling her fleshy nerve center as he pumped faster.

"God, that is so damn sexy, woman."

She barely acknowledged him as sensations overwhelmed her senses. Her bottom stung, one hand was on her hip, one on her breasts, each one caressing in turn as he continued to cycle in and out of her pussy. She was close, so close.

"Daddy," she said in a wispy voice. "Please, I want to come."

"Do it, come all over Daddy's cock."

His pace became punishing, and she held onto his forearm to further steady herself. The rush of passion, like a released dam, hit her hard, taking all cognitive thought. He moaned, panted, pumped, then stilled. She could swear she felt his release inside her, coating her walls and sliding down and out of her. She found herself laying on his chest, exchanging ragged breaths, mingling sweat, with the smell of sex permeating the air.

"That was incredible. You were incredible." He took another breath. "Cami, I was serious," he said as he moved her hair behind her ear looking into her very soul.

"Serious?" Her inflection exposed her confusion. "About what exactly?"

"Many things, but about this one thing in particular. I want to marry you."

Camille was quiet. "Is this you asking me? Like this? With me naked, sweaty and lying on top of you?"

"As unconventional as the rest of our lives have been, this is me, asking you to marry me. Soon. Quickly. We can do a reception later that you can plan as you like but let's just do it. I've waited so long to make you legally mine; I can't think about waiting any longer. The children need it legal. And we've made love several times, unprotected. I think you've proven it doesn't take much to knock you up. I want you and the kids to be taken care of if anything happens to me. I can list all the practical and impractical reasons, Camille, but it doesn't matter as much as I just want you because I love you."

"You done, cowboy?"

"I am if you're going to say yes."

"That was the best proposal I could've hoped for, cowboy. I love you so much. Yes, yes, I'll marry you."

He crushed her lips without warning, stealing her breath yet again. They made sweet love this time, napping a short time before dressing and entering the kitchen as Walker and Cody Race, their foreman, were sitting down to lunch.

"Hey, you two, thanks for standing in for me this morning. Looks like I'll be taking off again for a few hours. That something you can handle, Cody, because I told Walker he could leave early if he wanted? Marla will be here for Lily. We'll make a few stops, pick up Eli, and Camille and I are getting our marriage license. I imagine we'll be getting married Monday afternoon. I'm thinking seventy-three hours after we get into the clerk today."

The men congratulated Sawyer with hardy handshakes and back slaps. Cody politely congratulated Camille but Walker hugged her tight and kissed her cheek. "You know, that means you are getting all the Knight men in the bargain, right? Not this unofficial crap that you've had since you were a girl. This is real, forever."

Cami laughed and nodded. "I know. I'll get tips from Piper." Sawyer jumped in. "Okay, don't scare my woman off, Walker. See you Monday morning and thanks again, Cody. Let me know when you want a comp day."

Cody laughed. "I don't think that's a thing when you work a ranch."

"No? Yeah, you're probably right. Well, if you need some time off, you'll let us know and take it, right?"

"Always have, don't think I'll change now. You two get what you need done. We're quiet today."

Chapter 10

The officially engaged couple left for the courthouse, stopping to talk to Carole Dunlap, Belinda's daughter. She was hesitant in her congratulations, her words not reflected in her face, but Sawyer didn't seem to notice. Camille could see that the woman was waving a banner for Sawyer. She imagined she'd have to get used to it.

Thankfully, the court clerk was nice but an older woman who probably was used to seeing good-looking men waltz in and out of her office looking for marriage licenses. Not looking for any younger man to add to her collection, then. Good. She set up the justice of the peace for Monday afternoon.

"Let's stop at the attorney's office next. We can pick up the birth certificates while I get him to do a little more, then we'll have a late lunch."

Sawyer reintroduced Cami to the receptionist who was a year behind her in school. Camille noticed how this woman, as Carole had earlier, seemed to drool over her soon-to-be-husband and was less than joyful in their news. Again, her man was clueless.

Once in the attorney's private office, Sawyer laid out what he wanted. "Patrick, we stopped in for the birth certificates, and wondered if you could do a little more paperwork for us? I need my will changed to include Camille and the kids, and any other children we may have." The men talked while Cami sat and listened but didn't contribute. Her head was spinning with the events of the day. *My how the gossip would fly now.*

They decided to eat in the diner. After being seated and done placing their order, they chatted about all the things they needed to do. "We'll get rings after this."

"I don't need a ring, Sawyer."

"I do, and I can't have one if you don't, so doesn't look like you have a choice. Now, are we telling your parents?"

"Nope. I'll let them know afterwards when we invite people to the reception. I can't trust them not to try to throw a wrench in the works."

"If you're sure, then I should tell you something. What you walked in on with Belinda, she said she had heard a lot of it at bingo and it looks like the informant—"

"Is my mother. I figured as much. I don't know why she doesn't believe men with high-paying jobs still break the law. Are violent. Cheat. I have no idea where she gets her logic."

"Guilt. She feels guilty about you and if she pretends it didn't really happen the way it did, then she won't have to worry about atoning for her choices. Unfortunately, until she's dealt with her own issues on the subject, I can't let her near the children, alone. We can take them to visit her but that's it, no leaving them."

"I know. I don't think it's a problem because she hasn't asked."

"Probably more guilt."

"Who made you so smart?"

"I was born that way, sweetheart." He grinned arrogantly. Their meal was served, and he sobered. "Now, about harassment at the school."

Their discussion about the harassment took a while, but getting rings was fast and easy. She wanted simple, and he did as well. He got her something a little more than she wanted him to pay but it was beautiful. He considered taking her outside to explain how it was going to go but she backed down. She realized it was petty not to give him this moment.

Finally, it was time to walk into the superintendent's office. Camille was relieved when Sawyer sat next to her and held her hand, but he let her handle the situation. She was able to speak clearly and not cry. Sawyer's presence, and no interference, showed her how much she relied on him having her back but not fighting her battles. That felt good.

Old man Watkins kept giving Sawyer the side eye. His presence said all it needed to say. Camille was able to gain concessions from the superintendent. He'd issue a statement that unsubstantiated conversations about others not directly involved in the incident or incidents, as in eye-witnessed by the speaker, would be in violation of the ethical clause of their contract. The specific section could be found under modes of conduct. Any violators would find themselves liable for a lawsuit if found to be slander or libel. It could also risk immediate termination. It extended to all employees, students and encouraged familial compliance as well.

As they were walking out, Camille sighed in relief. "After Mr. Watkins turned a deaf ear to me this morning, it was gratifying to know that he could make the right decision."

"That and maybe your promise to go to the school board helped some, too. I believe it is his contract renewal year."

"Whatever works, I guess," she said and laughed as they neared the school administration's exit. She leaned into Sawyer. It felt good to have him with her. A familiar person approached as they were leaving the building.

"Karl, have you met my fiancé, Sawyer Knight?" The men shook hands. "Karl is the admin assistant who helped me get settled into the job. He's been a great help."

"Nice to meet you, Sawyer. I'm sure we've met somewhere in such a small town, but it's nice to meet you formally. Camille is an incredible nurse. She bandaged me up just the other day. Stopped the bleeding in no time flat."

She laughed. "It was a small but deep cut. I'm glad to have been of service. Please feel free to call on me for any of your nursing needs."

Karl started to say something when Camille's phone rang. She looked at the caller ID and then answered it. "It's the elementary school about Eli. We can go down this hall." She looked back at Karl as they started down the corridor. "See you later."

Entering the office together, Camille saw her son crying but trying his hardest to keep it to a minimum. Camille took in his swollen eye and bleeding nose and she headed straight for her son. She glanced at the obviously older boy seated across from him. When that child kicked at Eli's feet, Sawyer's booming voice echoed in the crowded space.

"That will be enough of that, young man."

"Sir, you cannot speak to a child that way. Not in this office," declared the secretary as she sat taller in her chair.

"Then do your job and keep him from kicking my son. I assume it was him that attacked Eli?" He asked the question but in a tone that said he already knew the answer.

"Eli doesn't have..." Obviously thinking better of her words, she glanced at Camille who wasn't paying attention to any conversation but the one she was having with Eli.

"Miss..."

"Moore. Mrs. Moore. And you are?"

"Sawyer Elijah Knight, Eli's father."

"What? Well... we... um..." Mrs. Moore looked over to Camille again, possibly in hopes of getting confirmation and reached over into a basket holding a file with Eli's name on it. Opening the file, she shook her head. "I don't have a birth certificate with your name on it, Mr. Knight."

"Am I listed as his father on the paperwork?"

"Yes, but..."

"Then that is all you need. Legally. But I can make things easier on you. Give me a moment."

He walked over and spoke to Camille. "Is he hurt enough to go to the emergency room?"

"No, I've checked him out, and it looks like a black eye, bruised nose, he might have a few more cuts and bruises but how does this happen to a five-year-old at school?"

Sawyer didn't know, but he was about to find out. He scooped up Eli in his arms and the boy settled onto his shoulder drawing his arms in under his torso. Sawyer didn't think he had ever been so furious in his life. Not even when he found out Cami had left town with another man.

"I'm going to get the birth certificates. You make sure the paperwork has all my information on there. Do it for Lily too." Camille nodded.

"Sir, Eli isn't allowed to leave..." The rest of the sentence died on her lips as she stared into Sawyer's face.

On their way out to his truck, Sawyer took some deep breaths, releasing as much anger as he could before speaking. "Are you okay, son?"

The boy nodded. Sawyer understood. Nodding was the best a man could do sometimes and keep his dignity. Returning with the originals, Sawyer stood as the woman took copies of the new certificates and under his watchful eye, she shredded the copies that were missing his name. Satisfied, he turned and sat next to Camille, still holding Eli close to his heart.

The principal said he was waiting on the boy's mother. They had a hard time getting either parent to respond but finally they reached the boy's mother. "Busy parents, you know," he said lamely. Turning to Camille, he said, "I'm so sorry about the misunderstanding this morning in the teachers' lounge."

Sawyer spoke up. He had had enough of the attacks on his family for one day. "Good to hear. Now was it the refusal to listen to her complaint that you're sorry about? Or that she had to go over your head? Or the pending school board complaint? Or maybe it was the blatant disregard of district ethical policy. Or possibly it's the common decency most people working with children should possess that you are apologizing for?"

Camille's hand landed on Sawyers clenched free one. "Sawyer, it won't help."

He took another deep breath blowing the air out forcefully. "You're right, but I'm fed up with people gossiping concerning things they have no idea about and wouldn't know the truth if it bit them in the–"

"Sawyer!"

Sawyer rubbed the back of his head. "It's just wrong, trying to ruin other people's reputations, allowing their children to hurt others physically as much as they do verbally. I don't intend to allow it any longer."

"Mr. Knight, if you are threatening the staff..."

"I can assure you that I'm threatening no one. What I am doing is promising there will be consequences, legal ones, if things don't change. I promise to take you to court if you don't make sure, on this property, that things cease immediately. My attorney is fully aware of the issue and he is keeping a nice little log of events and participants. My friend is a very good lawyer. He does our family ranches and confers with my sister-in-law's global firm, so you can imagine, a small defamation of character or assault case would be nothing."

It was obvious that the principal was grappling to respond but lucky for him, he didn't have to speak further on the subject. The mother to the little hooligan sitting on the bench walked in demanding to see her 'poor child' and proclaiming equally loudly that the bully who attacked her child would find himself sorry he had bothered with her offspring.

Camille started to let loose, but Sawyer knew because she worked for the district, she couldn't say anything. He didn't care if she didn't work at all off the ranch, just stayed home and raised the kids but she had struggled to get her degree and he knew what that meant to her. He wanted her to do what made her happy. Except right now. He gave her his sternest look and grabbed the hand she had placed on his fist earlier. She closed her eyes and struggled with its message of 'let me handle this'. She finally gave him a tiny, reluctant nod.

He squeezed her hand then let go. "Let's catalog the injuries first, shall we?"

Principal Keyes was actually a good man once Sawyer got past the fact that his five-year-old son was attacked on the playground. Keyes sifted through the ever-shifting sands of the story the third grader was telling. By the end of the talk, the third grader had exposed his parents' conversation in their home, causing the boy to believe Eli was a 'bad' kid because his mother was something called, 'loose'.

Sawyer spoke, leaving the room with no doubt that if his child was harmed in this way again, he'd be pressing charges and naming not only the parents but the school in the suit. That stopped all the snide remarks from the woman and had the principal assuring Eli and himself that it wouldn't happen again. Sawyer believed the man intended to do what he could to keep that promise.

Sawyer had dealt with enough of his community for one day. Time to go home. He led Camille out of the office while Eli dozed on his shoulder. As they walked up to the truck, something was odd. Cami must have noticed it as well because she cocked her head to the side, her 'tell' when she was puzzled. He loved that about her.

Her diminished tone spoke of her concern. "Did you trash the inside of your truck looking for the paperwork, Sawyer?"

"No, but it looks like someone did. Wonder what they were looking for?" He pushed the random garbage out of the way as he opened the back door and began to settle Eli into his seat.

"Did you have anything important in here?" he queried as he looked further inside.

"No. I brought my purse, that's it."

"Well, except for old garbage it's a non-issue. An annoyance at best."

"Oh, Sawyer, look at this."

Her tone, rather than her words, grabbed his attention. Looking at the glove box cover, written in lipstick, was the word, MINE.

"What the—" He scooped his now waking child back into his arms.

"Sawyer," Camille hissed. Her head tipped in the direction of their son.

He swallowed the expletive but allowed it and several others to scream around in his head. "Don't touch it. Back away from the door and let's call it in."

"I don't understand how this could have happened in the parking lot of the school."

"Honey, everyone and his brother comes to this building for one thing or another. It houses the community's children, and a percentage of the adult working population. Who knows? If there are prints, or the school cameras picked up anything we want there to be as much evidence as possible. So back away and go back inside. I'm calling Piper to come get you two."

"No way. She can grab Eli but I'm staying."

"Camille, you need to do as you're told this once."

"I'm not a child. I'm calling Piper but for Eli and to grab Lily so Marla can go home."

Piper arrived just as the police were and she spoke to Camille before leaving with Eli. The police had asked them to find another ride home, but Sawyer refused to leave his truck unattended. He wasn't leaving it exposed after the police were done.

Officer Randy Cambridge, a school buddy, shook his hand. "Sawyer, you always were the center of attention."

"Keeping up the family tradition. How've you been?"

"Yeah, good. You got a secret admirer, or did you buy a truck someone didn't want to part with?"

"Hell if I know, man. Camille has been saying the women drool over me, so, maybe it's the admirer angle. Had the truck a few years."

"You and Camille?" Randy looked over at the woman in question and nodded his head in her direction. "What about her?"

"What about her?" His friend couldn't know but he was over his quota of innuendoes and barbs at his family.

"Nothing. Just wondered if your admirer may have thought Camille was horning in on their territory."

Sawyer shook his head. "Can't think why? I've been just flitting these last years. Landing for a short stay and moving on. I wasn't seeing anyone when Cami came back with the kids."

He nodded. "Well, if you think of anything, let us know. And honestly, it's probably just some prank. Teens raising some hell. It's going to be awhile. Why don't you call someone to come and pick you up, then let us drive the truck back to you when we're done?" He glanced in Camille's direction. "Your girl looks tired."

Sawyer shook Randy's hand. "Yeah, it's been a long day. I think that's a good idea. Thanks, man."

Randy nodded towards the entrance to the school. "Looks like Jackson read my mind."

Sawyer laughed. "More like Piper called him. Thanks again."

Camille had already walked to Jackson who opened his arms and folded her into them. Sawyer would have been jealous if it weren't for the fact that his brother was happily married, and Camille had just picked up a marriage license with him. And if a whole long list of things didn't exist. He loved his girl and his brother and was glad for them both.

He slapped Jackson on the back. "Thanks for this. We could use a ride home. I'll tell you about our day on the way."

Chapter 11

The day she had longed for, the day she would become Mrs. Sawyer Knight had arrived after a whirlwind of weekend activity. Saturday, Piper insisted they go to Austin for a dress and regardless of her lack of enthusiasm at the start, Camille had enjoyed it. Josie had surprised the women by joining in the hunt for the perfect dress. They'd found a beauty in off-white satin and lace with blush-embroidered roses. It was simple and flowed gracefully to the floor. They'd found outfits for the children as well.

Sunday, Camille left Sawyer to deal with the children while she worked on salads and desserts for the barbeque. Sawyer decided they could grill after the 'I do's' and he invited employees from both ranches. Walker had tried to get Josie to come for the weekend through Monday, but she'd declined.

Monday afternoon was finally here. Although it had been a mere seventy-five hours since she had said yes to Sawyer, she found herself at the top of the steps with Eli, waiting for Sawyer to arrive. She in her delicate fairy dress and Eli in the first suit he'd ever owned, watching in nervous anticipation for their new life to begin. She'd opted to stay as long as she could at the school, dressing both herself and Eli in her full-sized bathroom in the nurse's office.

Camille's heartbeat quickened as she watched Sawyer carry Lily up the courthouse steps looking so handsome while talking earnestly to his young daughter. The petticoat enhanced pink confection worn by Lily, created a cloud of preschooler beauty in the arms of manly perfection. Josie, who had apparently changed her mind about attending the ceremony, walked up the steps behind Sawyer into the arms of Walker who had a grin as large as his brother's.

Camille checked the time on the large clock in the courtroom. It was three fifty-eight. In two minutes, the ceremony would begin. While Sawyer had said the license was good for ninety days, and she knew she could wait if she wanted to, Cami had no intentions of delaying this event any longer than she already had.

Looking at her handsome family, Camille wanted to relax, but she kept thinking something was going to happen that would stop her from getting this happily ever after. Cami thought Sawyer looked a little worried as well, but he tucked that away as soon as he realized she was watching him. He threw on a dazzling smile in response to her questioning stare, steering the children into their aunt and uncles arms. He then stood with Camille, his warm loving gaze encompassing her picture of bridal bliss made his eyes sparkle. The man practically sizzled in anticipation. It was just as she had imagined. Sawyer was it for Cami and as he looked at her with love and longing, she knew it was the same for him.

Their civil ceremony took ten minutes, including the signing of the certificate. They walked across the hallway and filed it, asking for a copy before they left the original. "Not necessary. Give me a minute to file it and I'll get you your official copy." When Cami's shocked expression met the older woman's, she continued. "It's the end of the day, no one's waiting. it's worth a few extra minutes. Congratulations."

The little group walked out of the courthouse forty-five minutes after walking in, headed home.

"It's your home now, Cami, forever," whispered Sawyer.

All she could do was smile. The feeling of worry over the event lessened but oddly, never actually went away. Telling herself she had worried for so long, being finally in a place of protection and safety was difficult to get used to, she did her best to dismiss the feelings of unease.

The ranch was overflowing with employees and their families.

Camille had called her parents after they left the courthouse, but her mother had said she was busy. Her father had said he should stay with her mother, but he did congratulate them. Camille cried over that.

"Cami, baby, I know it hurts. Honestly, I'm sorry it all happened this way and if you want a big wedding, we can do that."

Camille gave him her tear drenched smile and said, "No, really, it isn't that. I think we had a wonderful wedding. It's the vows that matter and our love, not how much money we spend, or how big a splash we make. It's about the life we make. It's just, they pushed me into something I had no business doing, and now, they're resistant to the one thing that will make me and the children the happiest. It's hard reconciling that reality with what being a parent means to me."

Sawyer gave her one of his heart stopping, curl your toes kisses. "They will come around and if they don't, we have to be happy in spite of their thinking. Now, speaking of which, where are our little munchkins? Piper wants pictures and I don't want to upset a pregnant woman."

Camille laughed, "No, sir, we do not want that."

The rest of the afternoon and evening was exactly how Camille had always envisioned life would be with Sawyer. After putting sleepy, complaining children to bed, Cami settled into his lap and snuggled in.

"It was great that Josie decided to come to the wedding."

"It was the best and I know it has everything to do with you and Piper including her on Saturday. Thank you for that. Walker has been trying to convince her they are the real deal, but she's still hesitant. Her history on the ranch and with Piper has been rocky."

"I heard some of the story and it takes time, but I think it will work out fine, so long as she is given support and we are unconditional in our acceptance of how she needs to proceed."

"Well, I think you're the best thing that happened to this place."

Camille laughed. "Yes, well, remember that the next time I don't agree with your high-handedness." Sighing, she continued. "I love the ranch because it was a part of you and all of you were so accepting from the beginning. Even after all I did, years later, you still accepted me."

"It's because they could see how much I loved you, have always loved you."

"More than half my lifetime."

The petting was getting heavier and the front room wasn't the place to make love. Not with children upstairs, a housekeeper sleeping on the same floor, and a brother back at any time.

"Come on, baby, I have plans for us and we need some privacy. I don't think you would be happy if one of the inhabitants walked in." He chuckled with an evil twist to his glee.

She imagined her husband would like nothing more than to be walked in on. He was an exhibitionist of the first order, and it was rare that he wore clothing in the often unlocked bedroom. She was shy, even with him at times, but she'd never be as comfortable in the nude as Sawyer always had been. Once he got her naked the first time, he seemed to lose all inhibitions. However, she had a strong suspicion he'd stayed clothed merely for her benefit until then.

Sawyer had waited until she was eighteen to take her virginity. He said she'd be an adult before he claimed her. He finally took her on her eighteenth birthday. A brand-new adult, but still legal. While she had been begging for months, he'd made her wait. When he'd taken her, on this very bed, he'd gone slowly. Done so gently.

She'd known he'd had other girls, but that had ended once she had entered high school. They were exclusive. Once he had taken her virginity, they were committed for life. She saw it that way even through the hard years and evidently, so did he because here they were, married. Sawyer was dominant even in the early years but more so once he'd claimed her innocence. It was part of his make-up and how the Knight boys had been raised. It was shortly after that she had called him Daddy.

Like that first time, Sawyer made slow, sweet love to commemorate their wedding. Touching her almost reverently, he anointed her with languid hot kisses that floated her into a magical nirvana. The climaxes were not violent, producing deep warmth that flowed over her frayed nerves and hyped emotions like a balm. He still controlled most of the play, but she was content to let him take her to paradise.

Making love with Sawyer, after they were married, held a different meaning now. Permanency. Security. Belonging. Things she had been missing since she'd left home and him. Things she had thought she might never find again. She snuggled into his embrace and slept.

The good thing about already having Sawyer's last name was now she only needed to add him to her employment paperwork. She changed the designation of those they could call from friends to sister and brother in laws and significant other to husband. The children's papers had been changed already. The whole day went by with some grumbling and some congratulations because nothing happened in this town without everyone knowing.

When she arrived at her car, ready to go home, she realized that putting a ring on her finger did not end the harassment. The act seemed to step up the annoyance, as Sawyer had called the lipstick incident. Now it had reached to the level of full vandalism. It was an unexpected backlash since Sawyer was taken off the market. That is if he could have been considered on it at all. And to whomever wanted him, Camille stood in their way. Her car had been spray painted with the word, 'MINE'. Quickly, she gave Eli the activity bag she kept in the car for times when she encountered a delay getting somewhere or for longer trips. With his inquisitive mind occupied, she called the police station and reported the vandalism.

"Hey, Camille, right? Weren't we here last Friday?"

"Yes. But lipstick isn't as difficult to remove as spray paint."

Officer Cambridge looked around the car and saw nothing out of the ordinary except her blue car had fire engine red spray paint on the driver's side. He whistled and shook his head. "Well, Miss Knight, it's going to be hard to locate anything that will help us find the culprit. We have found out that school cameras aren't that good this far from the building where the employees park."

"Well, do the report so I can get the insurance to cover the paint job, please. And it's Mrs. now."

He nodded with a knowing "Aha." Checking to make sure hers was the only car touched, he returned to where she and Eli were standing. "Sawyer coming to pick you up?"

"No, I'll just drive it home and figure out what next to do."

Randy shook his head. "I don't recommend that. You don't know if paint is all they did. Is there some reason this word was painted on both vehicles?"

She shrugged. "Kinda obvious, I guess. Someone is pretty upset that Sawyer is off the market. I came back to town and got back with Sawyer. Probably working through their disappointment. I can only imagine how upset they are now that we're married."

Randy whistled again. It was a little annoying. "Yeah, that might get a possessive woman riled up."

"Or a more rational one to stand down. Look in greener pastures." Camille sighed. "Okay, I need to get home if we're done here. I just need the report number so give me a call when you have it."

"You bet. You sure you don't want me to give Sawyer a call? I'm not real comfortable with you driving home without having a mechanic check it out first."

"You men are all alike. A woman can handle herself just fine. But thanks for your concern."

"I didn't mean to insult you." Randy seemed worried. "I'd have said it to anyone."

Camille laughed. "I'm married to Sawyer Knight and have the other Knights as my brothers-in-law. It's my daily life. I'm long past being insulted. See you later. Thanks for coming out when you heard the report."

"Any time." Officer Cambridge watched her as she climbed in the car and drove off. Camille smiled to herself. Dominant men.

The same thought crossed her mind again as she pulled in at the ranch. Evidently one hand saw the side of her car and before she had even finished changing, Sawyer came charging into the bedroom, allowing the door to slam shut.

"You didn't call me."

"Well, hello, Sawyer." She gave him a passing glance and then continued changing. "My day was great, thanks. That is until your son and I started for the car. I called the police station and your friend, Officer Cambridge, came out to look at things. It's not likely that they will figure out who did it but he's going to check the cameras, anyway. It's just that I park in the back as an employee so it isn't likely that they will be able to see well in that part of the lot. He's going to get me the report number so I can file it with the insurance company."

"Camille."

What was it about him using her name in such a way? She nearly fell apart. She knew she was too chatty but if she didn't continue thinking about the things ahead of her to do, she'd lose the race she was running. The race that took her from the emotional tidal wave of all the terrible gossip and now, the idea that someone thought her husband was stolen from some woman's hands. The fact that her child was subjected to the shock of seeing the graffiti on her car. And the bummer that he was learning to read.

"I have to pretreat the children's clothes so I can do the wash tonight. In fact, I should..." His hands anchored her, stopping any further movement away from him.

"Camilly Piccadilly, don't ignore Daddy." His voice was tender, and that made her angry because she was too close to tears without his gentleness. She needed his anger or his dominance, or something she could push against.

"Sweetheart, stop. I know what you're doing, and it won't work. You cannot chatter this away. We have to deal with it. I will deal with it."

"No, it is my problem, I have to handle it."

Sawyer was silent. Then, with her still in his hold, he walked them both to the door and locked it. She was led back to the bed, and he sat her next to him. Usually, if Sawyer was on the edge of the bed, she was not sitting but lying over his lap. Her apprehension must have shown. She watched his brows lift and angle, a sure indication that he was warning her.

"It is my job to keep you safe. I'll take you to school and pick you up every day until this thing is figured out."

"No, only until the car is repainted."

"Why are you fighting me on this?"

"Whoever is doing this isn't going to intimidate me. I won't be pushed out of my earned place because someone wants you and didn't get you."

"Excuse me?"

"You heard me. I won't be forced to do something I don't want to do again. It took years away from the man I loved. I'm done being a doormat."

"Is that what you think I reduce you to?"

"No. That isn't what I said. Don't personalize this, Sawyer. I love you and know you love me, but I am doing what I think is best." Her surprise at his misreading her must have been evident because he relaxed.

"Camille, anything to do with you is personal. Don't you understand?" He rubbed his hand over his face and took a deep breath, letting it out in a huff. He did it again only slower. "Okay, why aren't we discussing this instead of arguing?"

"I'm just stating facts. You're the one who won't accept my choices."

His voice dropped an octave sending the expected deep core reaction to gallop throughout her body. There was a warning in his voice when he spoke. "I'll tell you what I don't accept and that is you not calling me when you are in trouble. Not letting me know why you were an hour late. Why you thought handling this alone was the way to go when we're married, share a life, and the ups and downs in that life. That is what I won't ever accept and as your daddy, won't allow without retribution."

Chapter 12

Camille knew what was coming and her traitorous body gave in to it so easily. Her pussy was tingling and already lubricating. Her heartbeat was quickening, her breathing followed suit. She watched as if in slow motion as Sawyer settled more solidly on the corner edge of the mattress. He patted his knee and quirked one eyebrow.

She had relearned some of his most frequent nonverbal messages. Patting his knee was universal. Quirking an eyebrow was classic for *Are you sure you want to continue?* Both together meant he had had enough, and she needed to comply. The consequences of disobedience or pushing his already punched buttons at this juncture would be extremely inadvisable.

Still frustrated over the whole incident, she made a grave error she recognized right away but it was too late to rectify. Her dramatic sigh, which was equivalent to an eye roll or a refusal, was the final nail in her discipline coffin. Before another thought passed her backpedaling brain, she was unceremoniously tossed over Sawyer's muscular thighs that were anything but comfortable in this position. In almost the same span of time, he had the first round of swats plastered on her shocked butt. She gave over to him.

Sawyer shook his head in disbelief as his girl continued to defy him in the face of discipline. He expected her to whine, beg, offer a trade but instead she had incited his reaction. Landing the first round of solid swats, he could tell she was shocked it was happening. Maybe she hadn't reacted with intent, but she had tried to take on the problem this afternoon without even mentioning it to him in a phone call. That was clear intent to keep it to herself. The more he thought of the position she'd put herself and Eli in, the more determined he became that his girl understood, in no uncertain terms, when it was appropriate to handle something alone and when it wasn't.

He stopped to lecture as he slid his hands around her hips to the front of the jeans she had changed into a short while ago. He was glad she had submitted. It proved she needed it.

"These are in the way. My message isn't going to get through to you if my hand is smarting before we get down to the finale."

"Sawyer, no. Please. I'm sorry. I'm really sorry."

After he pulled her pants down, leaving her panties and most of her dignity in place, he laid his hand over her bottom and patted. "What are you sorry about, little girl?"

"Everything."

He landed four hard swats on her nylon and lace covered bottom. "Be more specific."

She groaned. "I ignored you when you wanted me to get into position."

He landed four more stinging swats.

"Not in the same place, Sawyer."

"I get more mileage out of the spanking if I do it my way. Now back to the ignoring part. You know better than to ignore me. So, tell me why you did it?"

"Because I don't like being told what to do."

Four more whacks landed on her bottom and he didn't need to hear her to know things were heating up on her lower quadrant. "Even so, was that any reason to throw me an attitude?"

"I didn't know I was until it had happened. I swear."

"I believe you so I'm only going to give you four more."

She sighed as he administered the next four smacks. Camille's hands began to climb up his calf to gain some leverage as she started to get up. "Just where do you think you're going?"

"What? I'm getting up. You're finished."

"With that portion. Now the real reason you are over my lap for punishment."

"What? Sawyer, no way. You can't punish me for being assertive and handling something as simple as vandalism. It was just one of your ex-girlfriends and that is not my fault."

"I can tell you it absolutely wasn't because I haven't had a serious girlfriend outside of you, ever."

"Well, it's obvious you weren't good in your communications because someone thinks I took you from them."

"Which could make them dangerous because it is clear someone isn't living in reality. And if that knowledge wasn't bad enough you stayed there waiting for the police to arrive instead of going back inside. Then, you kept Eli with you, exposing you both to possible risk."

"How do you know that?" she asked suspiciously.

"Got a call from Randy. He was checking to see if you made it home all right and thought I wouldn't appreciate him calling you directly. He was right."

Off went the panties and down came his hard hand bouncing off her bottom in sets of what he hoped felt like a thousand swats. The resulting sting, if he was doing this right, would be like bees were competing with wasps aimed at her butt without any way to get them satisfied so they would stop. At least he hoped that was the result. Camille had some home truths she needed to learn, the biggest one was she no longer did things alone. And this was fucking dangerous.

"Sawyer, too much. I get it." His girl was breathing hard, and he heard the break in her words as she spoke. He considered her statement. "Too much what?"

"Pounding on my ass."

"Evidently not because you aren't very respectful."

Another four strong swats later, she cried out, sniffling, "I'm sorry. I didn't think about the danger. It didn't seem like it with employees still there, but I was wrong. Please, honey, enough."

"I agree, enough."

Sawyer pulled her up, drew off her tee and bra, before laying her out on the bed. He took his time, looking his fill of his wife's body, so beautiful and lying naked before him, he unbuckled his belt and lowered his jeans until they hit his boots. Yanking off his boots, he cursed his lack of forethought, realizing he should have done that first. He saw her smile at his impatience when he ripped every stitch of clothing from his body.

Lowering himself to position his work-hardened frame around hers, he propped his arms on the bed and slid his thighs between her smooth ones, widening them, resting on his knees in the open vee it left for him. Placing his hands under her bottom, feeling the heat from her newly spanked flesh, his cock hardening at her whimper of tenderness, he centered himself and glided into place. Her moan this time was of satisfaction. His girl might complain, but spankings and hot bottoms fired all her rockets.

They would eat dinner soon, and this was not a good time roll for Camille, it was a 'who is the boss' act and those did not come with orgasms. It was evident his wife had other ideas because every pump in, she made little noises of being happily filled, and every pull out, she whined the loss. He picked up the pace and watched her movements and whimpers become more frenzied, his own need increasing with hers. Man, that was hot. He wouldn't last long.

"Naughty girls do not get to come, Cami." She gave him no response but as he savored the burn rampaging through his midsection and flames licked up every lust filled part of his body, she stiffened and came, dragging him off the cliff with her.

He wanted to be chastising, but it was the first time she had climaxed without so much as a tweak from him. She came from the psychological and physical heightening of her senses that the spanking and submission gave her. He'd point that out later. Right now, there was ten minutes until dinner was on the table, his wife was sound asleep, and his children needed rounding up.

Marla came at one p.m. on the dot and left with equal punctuality at six p.m. in the evening. Often Camille sent her home at five but not always and she was prepared to stay until dinner. Time to dress and change roles. Sawyer smiled. It was hard work and his life was considerably more complicated, but it was also fuller. He wouldn't change a thing, except the woman who had laid claim to him.

Camille had already claimed and homesteaded his property, but she needed to realize she wasn't alone any longer. The vandal, whoever the hell it was, would be found out soon, and he'd make sure she never bothered his girl again. As he prepared to leave the bedroom, he covered Cami with the fuzzy blanket she liked when she cuddled up with a book. He needed to talk to Walker and Jackson.

CAMILLE WALKED DOWN the stairs. It was seven, and she heard male voices coming from the kitchen table. Wandering in, she found all three Knight men with coffee, cake and whisky glasses.

"Did you leave any for me?" she asked with a smile.

Her bottom ached but at least she got sex, an orgasm and a nap out of the event. She wondered if Sawyer realized she had climaxed without his help. One look at his smug smile, and she guessed he did. The rat.

"Dinner, dessert, and coffee but sorry, no spirits for you."

"And why is that?"

"For the moment, because I said so."

Camille shrugged. "Good thing I'm not interested in it then, isn't it?" She looked in the oven and pulled out her plate, filled to overflowing with dinner. "Sorry I fell asleep. I must have been tired." Bringing her plate to the table but not yet sitting, she continued, "So, tell me why you men have gathered at this time of night in the middle of the week?"

Jackson, who was tact itself in public, was bold as brass with his family, of which she had been a member, officially and unofficially for close to fourteen years, responded in true Jackson manner.

"Wanted to see if Sawyer polished your butt well enough to stop you from dealing with things you should include your husband on, and if he's not available, one of your brothers. Camille, you know better, girl." He nodded in her direction. "By the way you're picking at your food from a standing position, I think that's my answer." He winked. Another rat in the house.

"Jackson, it's a wonder Piper puts up with you sometimes."

Jackson stood then, set his plate on the counter and folded her into one of those famous Knight hugs: warm... tight... real. He ended the hug by kissing the top of her head before stepping back and pushing her plate next to Sawyer.

Walker spoke then. "In all seriousness, Camille, you do need to involve one of us if Sawyer is unavailable."

"Except I was available."

"Fine, guys. I understand your egos were bruised when I didn't call in reinforcements, but I honestly didn't think anything about it. I've handled things alone since I left town."

"Good to know," said Sawyer. "But if you have the untamable desire to go it alone again, I'll just refresh that little reminder you're sitting gingerly on."

"Incredible. Good thing I've known you all well enough not to be embarrassed that you're lacking in all filters and social graces, so I don't expect it."

Walker chuckled. "Just so long as you do know what to expect, the rest will take care of itself."

"Including me. I'll call if necessary. I'm not reluctant, just self-sufficient and believe me, if I weren't, you all would be grumbling about that."

The chastising quieted as the men digressed, recalling the women who'd crossed their paths that were plain useless.

"Now," she started after finishing her dinner, "I need a little dessert and coffee before you tell me what you think is going on with this 'mine' business."

Other than agreeing it didn't have to be one of his recent dates, just someone who wanted a relationship with him, they were stuck. None of the women they knew seemed on the edge of psycho, and knowing the law's typical response outside of town, their expectations from that quadrant were extremely limited. They'd learned a lot since Piper's run-in with land developers. The best defense was a good offense, meaning the best result relied on Camille not exposing herself to anything or anyone that could be potentially dangerous.

"Well, I agree in theory but there isn't a person I know who would do this. At least I can't think of one," said Sawyer. "I mean why now? If it was the last one I dated for a few weeks, it was just a good time and we both agreed that was all it could be."

"So, she warmed your bed and nothing else."

Sawyer reached over and slapped her thigh. "Now who's without filters?"

Camille shrugged. She couldn't believe how jealous she was to know he did what she knew he did. He'd told her but somehow, it stung this time.

"I told you that was a while ago. Last winter."

"Sorry. So, if it isn't someone you've dated then how about someone who wanted to date you?"

"Hell, that'd be half the county," said Jackson.

"Available and unavailable," added Walker.

"Shut up. You two aren't helping me out any," ordered Sawyer.

"Actually, it's a good point," said Camille. "We won't be able to see who this did, based on these two incidents alone except it happened at the school, both times. Our common denominator."

Sawyer was frustrated. "And like I said, everyone and his brother goes to the campus for plenty of reasons."

"Okay, but why now? Why not when you were dating the last girl or the one before that?" asked Camille.

"Good point, actually," agreed Walker. "So, it must be when they believed it was serious."

Jackson added. "Or because of the kids. Everyone knew you were the kids' dad or at least it's what you were telling everyone. Or someone knew your history together."

Camille moaned. "In other words, the field is wide open."

"Afraid so. Look, I need to get back to Piper. She's been having difficulty sharing her workload."

"I think capable women are the bane of our existence," Sawyer said.

"Hush, you all love it," said Camille as she put the dishes in the sink.

Belinda didn't like anyone messing with her kitchen. Camille didn't push it. Times would change but for the moment she was content to let life settle around them. There wasn't room for any more conflict right now.

Jackson laughed. "We do."

"Yep," said Sawyer.

"Don't tell Josie, though. I'm already having the devil of a time watching out for her with her independent nature, and us living apart," Walker said with a hint of frustration. "And we agreed I wasn't settling obstinance with the methods we once used, what you now use. It makes it harder than it needs to be."

Waving to Jackson as he left the house, Camille turned to the man she had learned to love for his voice of reason and quiet comfort. His older brother was very different from her Sawyer, who was the youngest. In his teens and early twenties, Sawyer reacted first looking for the situation second. Recently however, since she had returned, he showed that his eldest brother was rubbing off on him. Maybe not so much today, but more times than not.

Jackson had the largest presence, Sawyer made the biggest splash, and Walker was the rock. She wondered if he felt like that with stalwart Josie who just forced herself to do things. Piper had said that when Josie was in her element, she was a powerhouse, but if she was uncertain, she'd force herself to continue. She pushed others away until she couldn't and then she'd walk away. Walker and she had indicated they pushed each other away often.

Walker because he wanted to shield her from harm, Josie because she made facing all obstacles mandatory, using sheer force of determination to overcome them. She took Walker's protection as a direct attack on her determination.

Walker defended her actions as due to her past, her childhood, her choices made before true consideration of the facts at hand. He had even taken the blame for some of it by saying he could overwhelm her by his forceful personality. That it sometimes put her in a tailspin, but Camille thought there was something much deeper going on than reckless choices and a misguided response to stress. Almost as though she was under pressure to make those choices under duress.

"Everything all right with Josie?"

"Yeah, she tends to take more risks than a single woman, my woman, should take."

"I think that might be coming to an end soon. Josie seems smitten with you, but she doesn't know how to have a man as confident as you. She's done things on her own for so long, giving in and turning over some of the responsibility or at least sharing it will be a learning experience. I expect you already know that, though. She'll learn a happy balance and so will you. She wants the feel of you taking care of her but the actual event of you doing that, isn't something she'll easily allow to happen consistently."

"Sounds like someone else we all know," Sawyer pointed out.

"I have children to mellow me, open me to possibilities. Josie doesn't."

"I'd rather win her before we have any kids, though."

"Hey, don't knock it."

"Hush, Sawyer, Walker is right. If you want to win her to the ranch, which she says she's loved since coming here, it's like you do trailer loading a jumpy horse. You lead them in with the side door open, so they think there's always an out along the way. Then, when they're in, you distract them and shut the door."

"Now who's using equestrian analogies?" Sawyer leaned in to kiss Camille. "I think it won't be long until we have another woman on this place, filling it with babies."

"That's another thing I wanted to talk to you about. Josie came from a large family and she isn't keen on having more than two. I thought I'd build a place on the south corner where it's wooded and not using up good pastureland."

Camille spoke with confidence and firmness. "You are the eldest and by rights, we should build something else. We are not pushing you out of this house."

Walker dropped a kiss on Camille's forehead as he stood to put his glass in the sink. "Thank you, sweetheart but you wouldn't be. It just makes more sense. Besides, you've practically grown up here. It's as much your home as any of ours. Josie doesn't have history here and wouldn't mind having her own place. Might even prefer it. We aren't there yet but it might be the carrot she needs to make the move. Think about it. Night you two."

Chapter 13

"I'm not doing it, Sawyer. Now we need to get to school. I'll talk to you later."

Camille shot her husband the look he had christened the 'defiant' look, and he bit his tongue. Lily had the same look when she refused to do as she was told. He put Lily in the corner to rethink her decisions when he encountered that look from her. He wanted to put her mother in the corner often as well, but with the addition of a hot bottom. Problem was, they didn't live alone. He had to relegate all those types of responses for the seclusion of their bedroom. Maybe that was a good thing.

Sawyer knew Camille was concerned with the two acts of vandalism, but she also had decided in her head that there would be no more incidents. The car had been repainted. There'd been no other juvenile painting of the word 'mine' on any item belonging to them since then. She was driving to school and no matter how many ways he told her he didn't think it was a safe thing to do; she was going to do it.

Jackson and Walker had convinced him he couldn't just take over her life, no matter how much he wanted to do that. "You have to watch from the sidelines and be vigilant, available. She is her own woman and if you suffocate her, she'll rebel."

"You mean more than she is now?"

"God, yes," said Jackson. "She is ultra-compliant compared to Piper on some days. Promise me you'll give her some space."

Walker laughed. "Or rope. You can come in to rescue her when she's about to truss herself up with it."

Sawyer shook his head. "I want to keep her safe more than teach a lesson about following my direction."

Walker sobered. "I know. Bad joke. Sorry. I would suggest she park in the front in view of the camera."

And that is what Sawyer had demanded in a compromise and she'd jumped at it. He had to believe she'd be safe. He checked in at lunch and things were good. She sent him a text at the end of the school day, saying they were on their way home. The routine was established with no other incidents. Halloween was approaching, and the children were getting excited. With energized kids, the school had more incidents of bumps, bruises and careless mistakes leading to small injuries. While they weren't technically challenging, they were increasing her workload. Sometime in the week prior to Halloween, the phone calls and texts diminished to none by the time they arrived at Friday, October 31st. Halloween.

Sawyer used to love this holiday as a kid. Dress up was fun, but the scare factor, the bit that was everywhere and got the adrenalin pumping was not to be missed. Camille had been grappling with Eli's choices of costumes. Lily wanted to be a fairy princess and no amount of alternative costumes suggested by Eli, Sawyer or her uncles could change her mind.

"I think you have undue influence on Lily," accused Sawyer.

Camille laughed. "Why do you think that is? Because I'm her mother, a girl, or because I think her choice is a good one?"

"All the above. I want to lodge a formal complaint."

"Oh, yes? Then I would like to lodge the same. My five-year-old son, who was happy to be a superhero last year, insists on being a werewolf this year. No small thanks to you and your brothers."

"Now, hold on. He brought that idea to me. I just approved it."

"Without asking me."

"Yep. Baby, it's a costume, not a career or lifestyle choice. I bet he'll find he doesn't like it as much as the superheroes and he will be one of those again next year."

"Or Dracula. Or the walking dead."

Sawyer drew her close and kissed the woman he grew to love deeper every day. "I love you, Camille Knight, and I love that you worry about every aspect of our children's lives. But let me have this one concession."

"Well, it's too late to change our minds now anyway, but if anything happens to cause him to have nightmares, you, Mr. Knight, will be on the sofa for the foreseeable future."

"Yeah, well, we'll need to negotiate that consequence." He dropped another kiss on her lips. "Let's get our wolf and princess dressed so we can start. We have a lot of areas to cover. Josie and Walker are coming over tomorrow. We thought we'd cook out since the weather should be mild. You know, have an easy weekend."

"A low-key weekend. I can't wait."

Three hours later, Camille, Sawyer and two weary children, costumes in disarray, stumbled into the house. Camille had donated candy to the joint fire/police event where they distributed candy and treats along with showing cartoons, some games, and took pictures for the community. Then, Sawyer had plenty of places he wanted to stop as much to show off his family as to gain more candy for the children. Camille sighed as they entered the house, relieved tomorrow was Saturday. She stripped the kids in the kitchen, helped them brush their teeth and threw jammies on them before sleep overtook their little bodies.

Taking both bags of candy, Camille sat on the floor and dumped one out in front of her.

"What're you doing?"

"Going through the candy to make sure it's safe before I turn the kids loose on it."

"You don't have to do that, it's safe. We live in a small community. We know just about everyone."

"Sorry, I know you're right. I need to do it for my peace of mind, though. And obviously there was someone who wasn't happy with the Knights."

"Okay, give me Eli's and I'll go through his."

After looking through the first bag and finding nothing, Cami put it all back in and declared Lily's bag child ready. Sawyer couldn't say the same for Eli's bag, the contents of which was still on the floor in front of him. He'd dumped it out as he'd seen Cami do. After swishing the wrapped candy around on the carpet looking for defective wrappers, Sawyer began to put the cleared sweets back in the bag when he came upon a folded piece of paper. Thinking his son had picked it up from somewhere or it was from school, Eli was always gathering things and putting them in his pocket, he opened it to see what treasure lay inside.

The paper unfolded to hold one word 'MINE'. Sawyer was still processing where he'd found it when Camille laughed.

"You don't have to do more than make sure the wrapper is unopened and things look untampered with." She stopped. "What is it you have there?"

He had no more time than to look up into her face and back down at the paper before she whispered. "Where did that come from, Sawyer?"

He laid the paper carefully on top of the spread candy. "Inside Eli's bag."

"Sawyer. That means whoever is doing this was close enough to our son to put it in his bag."

Sawyer's face and tone was grim. He called the sheriff and Jackson. Jackson arrived first.

"Piper was already asleep, or I've no doubt she would've come with me."

"No, no that's okay," said Sawyer. "Camille ran up to check on the kids." He stared at the paper still lying on top of the candy. "It's much more personal now, Jack. They targeted my son as the messenger. The trouble is, other than the obvious fact that we saw and passed half the community tonight, the message has been the same. Same word in bold fiery letters. Who have I dated that is so crazy as to do this?"

Two sheriff's deputies knocked on the door and soon asked the same question. "I admit I wasn't the most discreet person in the last few years, but I was always up front about my inability to do more than hook ups."

"Anyone difficult to shake off when things were over? Anyone not willing to take you at your word?"

Jackson perked up. "There was one, Sawyer, that Susan Dawkins. Remember?"

"I do, but that was over a year ago and she's married with a baby on the way. Susan Miller, now." Things were silent. The deputy turned to Camille who had remained uncharacteristically quiet.

"Mrs. Knight, have you had any trouble with a woman saying snide remarks or making statements that your husband had made a mistake, or was taken, or anything like that?"

Camille gave him an incredulous look and said, "If you don't know the answer to that question, Deputy, you're the only one in town that doesn't."

"Excuse me?"

Sawyer cautioned. "Camille."

She ignored him. "Half the town has said it to my face or behind my back or in some way implied it since I arrived back home. It seems I'm a gold digger, a bewitcher, an adulteress, a man stealer and any number of other delightful things. Really, you should hang out at any place women are to get more up on the goings on in town. You shouldn't be the last to know."

Sawyer's hand landed on Camille's, but she shook him off.

He reached again, and this time held on tight. "I think what my wife means to say is she has been the subject of some intensely hurtful gossip."

"What she means to say is that my husband walks by a woman and nine out of ten times, that woman is watching him walk away. The more he saunters, the longer they look."

"Ma'am, I don't think... Are all these women unmarried?"

"Who the hell knows. But I do know one thing, which is that she, whoever she is, got so close to my baby that she could and did put that paper in his trick or treat bag. I guess we don't have to guess whether it was a trick or a treat." Camille stood and stomped to the kitchen.

Sawyer was torn between going to see his girl or finishing off the interview. Deciding it was better to give her time to settle down he stayed and finished the interview. Seeing the deputies to the door, Sawyer sat down to think how he should approach the situation with Cami, when she walked back into the room and curled up in his lap. He hadn't realized how concerned he was until she came to him for comfort. His entire being relaxed.

Jackson stayed a while longer brainstorming with Sawyer on how they could combat these things. "The deputy is right. We can't keep the kids in a bubble and there hasn't been any harm to a person, just that one damn word used strategically to scare us."

"Not us. Me," said Camille.

Jackson stood and kissed the top of Camille's head, then ran his hand down her hair in comfort. "Let's think on this and after chores in the morning, we'll see what we can come up with. Walker and Josie will be here tomorrow afternoon. We'll figure something out."

Sawyer nodded. "Sounds good."

Sawyer picked up Camille and carried her towards the stairs. "Sawyer, I'm too heavy." He landed a light but noticeable smack on her thigh and then threw her over his shoulder. "What are you doing?" she asked in a stage whisper.

"Taking my wife to bed. Now if you have a problem with that, I would love to teach you what happens to naughty little girls who do not listen to their daddy."

"We will be heard!" she said in those same hushed tones.

"Nah. I'm willing to take a chance. Belinda is at her sister's this weekend. The children sleep like logs, and Walker is gone tonight."

At the top of the stairs, he stopped and changed direction, going to the children's room. While still holding onto her, he opened the door and peeked into the room. Their cherub faces were serene. He wished he slept like they did. He reached down and pulled the blanket up over them then turned to leave, waiting while she got a good look at her babies before taking his girl to bed.

The next morning, waking satiated and content in her lover's arms, Camille snuggled deeper in his embrace. He moved to accommodate her as he reached to cup a breast. She tried to shy away from that level of intimacy with an immediate response.

"Don't."

One word. It was so powerful, sending ripples of pleasurable anticipation through her body followed by anxious trepidation. That thought led to remembering the one word that had dominated their time together last night. Their lovemaking was so desperate as though the more intense their coupling, the less power that damn word had over their lives. Now, when she should allow herself to drift back to sleep, that word: 'MINE' seeped into her psyche and took over her mind. It made her angry the power one word had over her happiness, and it was going to stop, dammit. It had no more power over her than she let it. He is MINE not YOURS! Her brain screamed in the dark. Whoever the hell she was!

Sawyer moved next to her, drawing her closer to his heat.

"Make love to me."

Without a word, he raised over her pleading body. With intense blue eyes stormy with emotion, he lowered his mouth to hers. She tangled her fingers in his longish hair and pulled him into her, held him tight, and rode the wave of his love. Kissing downward, he hovered over erogenous areas she never realized existed, the curve of her waist, the concave of her hips, her mons, each tease of his lips and tongue heightened her center already vibrating with sensitivity.

Her blushed skin heated to inferno levels as he continued his slow descent. She released her hold on his shoulder and head as he dropped lower. Fingers tangled in his hair again as he lavished his gentle loving on her. He nipped, and she squirmed. He tongued, she moaned. When he barged the gates of her pink fleshy bits, she cried out. It felt so good. Erotic.

His mouth, tongue, raspy beard all teased her senses, drawing out the liquid arousal from her, raising her desperation to be filled by her man even higher. First one finger tested her readiness for him, then another, her molten emotions seeping from its chamber onto his hand. She could feel her ache increase, his thumb found her nerve center, sending signals of pleasure to her core, drawing out the passion that had lay in wait for their next release.

Now the one hand, drenched with her essence, was encircling her sensitive back button, breaching her rear entrance. She craved his domination. He slid in another finger to stretch her passage. In, out, expand... in, out, expand. The fires of arousal were stoked higher and higher as she raced to the finish line of satisfaction. Another finger was introduced. Three now danced rhythmically in, out, then expanded in the small space only to repeat the movement. Unfamiliarity mixed with the forbidden and a touch of pain, was more than she could bear for long. She couldn't hold off her climax any longer and yet it teetered on the precipice not quite falling over.

He did something he had never done before. He forced in a fourth finger simultaneously saying, "Now."

That was all. The combination of too much, not enough, a distinct slice of pain and his command sent her over the edge of sanity into a world of kaleidoscopic flight. He removed his backend intrusion and slid his erection into her sweet center and took what was only his. What she gave to him freely as she bound him to her forever.

MINE.

Chapter 14

Sunshine shone through the cracks of the curtain. It took a moment for Camille to come up from the deep dregs of her sleep. Rolling over to look at the clock, she moaned in the delicious ache that came from a long night of sweet rabid sex. Gentle, frantic, dominant, and indulgent loving were all ways she'd have described her night of debauchery with her husband. Camille giggled. Was it debauchery if it was with your husband? If it wasn't, then it felt decadently wicked at times.

The shocking cold from the floor raced up her legs producing one violent shiver that encouraged her to dash to the bathroom. Getting a carpet for the floor around the bed just shot to the top of the list of needs. Soon she was warm and energized from the heat of the shower. An obviously male hand, roughened from hard manual labor, landed on her warm wet rear.

"Hey, that's deadly. New shower rule, no swats."

"But I owe you a spanking for last night. I had decided to delay it until today. With the kids watching cartoons, I figured two birds-one stone."

"No way, buster. That really hurts. Besides, I didn't earn one yesterday."

"Five. Right now. Done."

Something told her that even five would be too much for her in the shower. She changed her response tactic. "Daddy, showers should make you feel good."

His slow smile should have enlightened her, but it didn't.

"Oh, I can make it feel so good."

"And the spanking? That will feel good as well?"

"No, the spanking will hurt because you disobeyed when I warned you to settle down last night. But I will make you forget the sting. Five now and shower sex, or ten later, no sex."

"Fine!"

"Attitude will get you more. Do you want to answer me again?"

He tweaked her nipple lowering his head to enclose it in her mouth. Her core tingled, creating liquid arousal.

"Sorry, Daddy. Please spank me kindly, then make love to me."

He chuckled. "Spank you kindly? Cute, and shower sex is not making love, its hot, heavy, pressurized sex, baby. It's what you want after your spankings. Lean into me."

He was right, damn him, but oh my God. After the first wet swat echoed off the shower walls, Camille was trying to change her mind. Sneaky man that she had married, landed four more hard smacks causing tears to fill her eyes before she could beg off or try to breathe through them. The last ringing slap hadn't silenced before her mouth was covered by his, seeking gratification. He turned Camille, planted her hands on the shower wall, and entered her hard. She loved the rougher sex after a nasty spanking. Her body throbbed with a primal need. She could come after discipline, when he allowed, but she needed to ask.

"Please let me come." He pounded without answering. "Sawyer, I'm so close."

He bounced his hot hand on her wet flank. She hissed. "Spread your legs more."

She did. "Please, Sawyer." Another swat. She gritted her teeth.

"What do you call me when we're like this?"

"Sadist?" She moaned at the ensuing swat. "Daddy! I call you daddy." Her voice was rife with anguish. "Let me come." She was begging, and she didn't care.

His hand landed on her spread pussy as he said, "Come."

He called those little evil slaps 'pussy pats' and 'clit claps' according to which he used. She didn't need direct stimulation at a time like this. His swat stung just enough to put her over when she was on the cusp of orgasm. Her man knew her so well that the exact moment when she teetered was perfectly timed with his pat. Over she went as he buried himself deeply inside, pumping hard. His hand covered her mouth as she cried out.

"I love you, Camille Knight."

His guttural noise signaled his release right behind her. The day had begun.

It was late morning when Piper came over while Jackson was still doing his chores. "I have to come when I'm between things or I get going on a project and lose track of time."

"I understand that. You have so many things going at the same time, I'm amazed you can take a break."

Piper shrugged as she reached for another potato to peel. "No big deal, really. I have office help and a vice president, but I still get tangled up in things easily. Guess I'll have to hire a nanny when this little squirrel is born."

"I suppose. Don't you wish you could just stay home and take care of things there?"

"You mean like a housewife and mother? Nope. I love my business and working on the administration part with Walker over the ranches, but I did want children. It was a little surprise but only timing wise. I plan everything out and this was not due to happen until next year. I'm flexible though." She smiled and Camille had no trouble believing her.

"Now, you I would peg for being the stay-at-home mom."

"I'd love it, but I also enjoy nursing. This is the best of both worlds right now. If we decide to have another baby, then I'd eventually have to re-evaluate, but for now, it's perfect."

"I can't imagine Sawyer not wanting to be with you through at least one pregnancy. These guys are funny like that. Just like they are funny about their wives getting harassed or bothered." Piper continued when Camille didn't fill in the silence. "When Blackwell Investments began to bother me and then that Lathrop guy got personal, and deadly, these guys all but put me in a locked room."

"I heard about that. I can't believe someone burned down your apartment building and then tried to shoot you. But what I had a hard time believing is that you used yourself as bait. Did you ever sit after that escapade?"

"Not for a long time. Yeah, not my brightest moment and I regretted it daily for about a month. Even longer than that with Josie and Walker. I lost her as a friend and an employee. Walker lost her as a girlfriend for a while. He wasn't happy with me either."

"But you're okay now, right? I mean Walker talks about you as a sister and Josie went dress shopping and other things since. So, I hope that means it's all good."

"I think so, with Walker anyway. Josie went dress shopping because she hadn't met you and I'm sure she was curious."

Camille handed a cherry to Lily who was trying her hardest to get a taste of the goodies they were preparing. "I think things were good with Josie at the wedding cookout."

"The best they have been, really. But just to be on the safe side, don't mention anything about the Blackwell Incident."

"Got it. Lily, out. You are as bad as your father."

"Daddy's not bad. He's funny."

"You're right. I bet he is looking for you to play with him."

"Nope, he said boys play with boys and girls play with girls."

"Lily, I don't think Daddy would say that."

Boots sounded on the wooden floor. "Oh, yes he would. Miss Lily forgot to add that she was running after the ball and then refusing to kick it or give it back so the rest could play."

"That's because I want to ride my pony."

"What pony?" asked Camille.

For once, her husband looked sheepish and before he could answer, Lily piped in. "The pony Daddy gave me. She's so pretty."

"I see." It was Camille's turn to look sternly at her husband. "How long ago was this?"

Sawyer addressed his daughter. "Lily, go outside. We have to eat before we ride."

Lily stomped her displeasure. "And that, my little lady, will get you five minutes in the choices chair."

The waterworks began but Sawyer never faltered. He placed her in the corner seat and set the timer next to the chair. She knew when the timer went off, she needed only to apologize specifically and off she could go. It had been Camille's method, and she was happy he had subscribed to it so easily. There were times he deviated and used more concrete methods as did she, but in this house, Camille was the only paddled one.

Camille left Piper in charge of the preparations while she led Sawyer into the family room. "Now when did you give her a pony?"

"Today. Eli too."

"That is something we should have discussed."

"I understand and you're right, but they were getting the ponies. We live on a ranch where cattle and horses are commonplace. I work with horses or have something to do with them every day. It's time they start settling into a saddle."

"I didn't agree."

"No, you didn't, and I should have told you how I felt about this whole issue. You're going to ride again as well."

"I think I'll wait until the summer if you don't mind. That way, if I fall off, I won't be cold and bruised. It hurts more in the winter."

Sawyer laughed and pulled her in for a kiss. "Something crossed my mind when I was introducing the kids to their ponies. Lily's is perfect, by the way. She's a pretty Paint. Anyway, I was thinking about our next child and—"

"Next child?"

"Yep. Now the horses got me thinking about the next one and then that took me to sex, which took me to the realization that I'd not used a condom most times. And I wondered what birth control method you used."

"Oh. Yeah, well I got the implant even though I didn't expect to have sex. That thinking hadn't always worked well for me, so..." She shrugged.

"Great. When do we need to look at our options?"

She sat on the couch with a bounce. "Lily turned four mid-July, and I had the implant put in when she was born."

"Okay, and how long does it last?"

"Four years?"

"Does that mean you can't remember, or you got it when she turned four, or we should have been using something since Lily's fourth birthday? Meaning every time we made love."

"Yes, that one."

"Which one?"

Camille turned tear-filled eyes to his. "Sawyer, I'm so sorry," she whispered. "I was distracted with the move and the trouble with Mom, then you came along. And since I haven't had sex, and I didn't need to think about birth control regardless, it slipped my mind that the time had passed."

Sawyer sat down next to Camille. "Honey, it's all right but are you saying you needed another implant when Lily turned four?"

"Yes."

"Gotcha. Well, first thing is we need to get a test to make sure you aren't pregnant and then work on addressing where we are then."

"I didn't try to trap you or do this on purpose."

"Hey, where did that come from? We were both responsible for birth control. Neither of us used protection most of the time."

"But we haven't even talked about whether we want more children and if so, when? It's so irresponsible."

Sawyer kissed her lightly. "I agree. I should have thought about it every time. And I always have with anyone else, I swear. But with you, I can't think about anything but getting inside of you and hearing you scream." He took her hands in his. "If we're pregnant, then we are. If we aren't, then we get a chance to plan. I want as many children as you will give me, Cami. No stressing over this though. What's done is done. We deal with what is laid before us."

Hearing him use the plural in the conversation lessened her concern. He'd be right there with her if and when they had another child. "Right, but at least I don't feel pregnant. I count that as a good sign."

He kissed her cheek but didn't answer. Camille was amazed it didn't dawn on her to think about birth control. Sawyer was right, what was done was done, but still.

Sawyer looked in the direction of the choices chair. "I think Lily has taken off to parts unknown since her time in the chair is long up."

"She's a smart girl."

"Like her Mama." He dropped another kiss on her lips. "Now I think I hear Walker in the other room. Let's go have some fun. We'll deal with the question of a baby later." Camille nodded in agreement.

Knowing what she did about Josie's time on the ranches and her decision to leave the ranch, Piper's employ, and for a while, out from Walker's protective shadow, Camille tried hard to keep things away from that time. She expected Josie to be quiet with the other two men, but nothing could have been further from the truth. She was engaging and relaxed.

After dinner, as the children played in the yard, something they never seemed to tire off, the subject of the vandalism came up with the adults. Jackson led the conversation right into last night's Halloween fiasco.

"You mean someone came right up to your Eli and gave him that paper?" asked Josie.

"You know, I had assumed that they had thrown it in his bag, but she might have given it to him. Let's ask him," said Walker. The guys walked outside and while playing around with the kids, asked Eli what he knew. When they walked back in, there was more concern on their faces than when they left.

"So?" asked Camille.

"Eli said he didn't know it was in his bag but something odd did happen. I'm not sure you want to hear it." Sawyer's face was grim.

"Just say it," said Camille but she wasn't sure she wanted to hear it either.

"The paper wasn't put in Eli's bag at first. It was dropped in Lily's."

"What?" asked all the women at once.

Piper glanced at a stunned Camille before speaking up. "How do you know?"

"Because Lily said she didn't want it in her bag, so she threw it in his."

"Does she know who gave it to her?" asked Josie.

"She's four," said Camille.

"Actually, she knows when it was put in her bag just not by whom," answered Walker. "She got it at the fire station. She saw it in her bag right after they gave her candy."

"Did she know who the lady was or what she looked like?" Camille asked.

Sawyer shook his head. "Nope, she just said it was a fire guy with candy."

"That's no help," said Piper.

"I disagree, honey. It says one of the people giving out candy at the fire station stop did it," said Jackson.

"I don't know. There were an awful lot of people there. She even said she didn't like it because people were pushing. I still think anyone could have done it."

"I think Camille is right," said Josie.

Piper sighed. "I agree. It's just not enough."

"But that means whoever it is knows who Lily is and doesn't mind using children to get their message communicated. Sawyer, maybe we should keep them home."

"I'm all for that but do you really think someone would hurt one of the kids?"

Walker spoke up. "I don't want to make it less than it is because I'm flaming that someone would use a little child for something like that, but I don't think they're in danger. I mean, they're trying to get the adults' attention, but they believe it's Camille's fault not the children's fault."

"I'm not sure I agree but I want to," said Camille. "Sawyer, we better keep them home."

"Baby, Eli will pitch a fit and Lily is only there for a few hours. How about we just keep a closer eye on them for now? It's you I'm more worried about."

"I'm fine."

Sawyer looked at the other two couples in the room. "We think she might be pregnant."

"Sawyer, that's premature. We don't even know yet. We've just discussed the possibility."

"I know, baby, but this is our family and they won't tell anyone else until we confirm it and not even then until we are ready to announce it. I just need everyone on the same page, and this makes you more vulnerable."

"If I'm pregnant, and that's a big 'if', it will make me puke more, not weaker."

"Cami, I didn't say weak. More susceptible to being hurt. Not at all the same thing."

They discussed the safeguards they needed to put in place, but Camille was rejecting all ideas.

"Listen." She stopped the chatter. "I'm parking in front. I'm coming after plenty of others have arrived and I'm leaving as soon as I can after work. It's the best I can do right now."

Jackson added, "And don't go anywhere alone."

"Fine, if I can help it, I won't. I can't promise that there aren't things I'll have to do without an escort, but I promise to be extremely careful." Sawyer began to open his mouth. Camille put her hand up to forestall his next words. "Sawyer, I can't promise more."

Walker added. "She's right, Sawyer. But I want the children with adults at all times when off this ranch. There are no play dates or whatever the hell they call those things, and no birthday parties that someone doesn't stay with them."

Everyone agreed. They moved on to play cards for a while. When Camille decided it was getting too late for the children to play outside, she brought them in and allowed them to watch a movie in the den. After another hour, Jackson and Piper went home because she was tired. Josie decided to stay the night, much to Walker's delight, and Camille put the children to bed.

Later than night as Sawyer and Camille were getting ready for bed, she sighed. "I'm glad Walker and Josie are doing better."

"Yeah. He's taken with her but I'm not so sure she's taken with the idea of making it more permanent."

"It takes time. You Knight men are a little hard to get used to. I mean, Piper and I have known you most, if not all, of our lives. Josie hasn't had that opportunity to get used to you."

"We are, are we? Well, let me help this woman feel more comfortable with her man."

She giggled. "Okay, let's see if that's even possible, Mr. Knight."

"Yes, ma'am," he said as he rushed her and tossed her on their bed to her squeals and giggles.

MONDAY SEEMED HARDER than most to get the day started. Camille worried about exposing the children to the world of stupid people, but they did the whole week without incident. By the following Monday, things were much easier and with no further incidents, Camille focused on her doctor's appointment. There weren't any appointments after three p.m. as he saved those for children, so as much as she hated it, she had to send a request to come in late and take the first appointment of the day.

She was a district employee so sending her request to the district office meant a longer wait for an answer. She'd barely received the approval before the day of the appointment. Karl dropped by the afternoon before her appointment to confirm receipt.

"Hey, did you get your approved leave slip?" he asked.

"I did. I was sweating it a little," laughed Camille.

"Nah. You're not sick, are you?"

"Nope. Just getting something checked out."

"Not serious I hope," asked Karl.

"Not at all. Thanks for asking. Sorry to cut you off, but I have to get these new student health records checked before I go home. Thanks again for following up on the paperwork."

"I wish everyone was that nice," Camille grumbled to herself.

As Camille drove onto the ranch, she saw someone showing something to Sawyer. Their heads were bowed close together, intently poring over whatever was in their hands. Coming closer, she could see it was Carole Dunlap. She felt her green-eyed monster rising up to spew meanness from her mouth. She took some deep breaths.

Sawyer only had eyes for her. But Carole, on the other hand, only had eyes for him, it would seem. Was Carole the jealous person trying to claim her husband? Cami decided she needed to make sure to stake her claim openly. She shooed Eli out of the car who was anxious to check on his horse. Once he had scampered off, Cami slammed the car door a little too hard and walked up to the pair, sliding her arm around Sawyer, flanking his left side.

"Hi, handsome. Whatcha looking at?"

He kissed her lips lightly. "Carole brought over some garden ideas. I thought it would be nice if we tried to spruce the place up more since we have more than me and Walker here. She has a landscape business and brought me over something to look at."

"Oh, that's nice."

Cami looked over at Carole who seemed to have an odd expression on her face. Something between smugness and jealousy. An odd mix and Cami almost laughed out loud until she realized that this could be the woman who wanted her husband enough to vandalize and put things in her children's Halloween bags.

"Carole, did I see you on Halloween passing out candy with the fire department?"

"Yep, been doing it for a few years." She looked over at Sawyer. "You guys should volunteer again, Sawyer."

He seemed to consider it. "I might think about it when things settle down here a bit."

Camille spoke up. "Carole, if you could leave your plans and suggestions here with us tonight, we'd have some time to look them over. Give them the attention they deserve."

Sawyer jumped on the idea and Carole threw Cami an irritated look. Camille smiled, seemingly as unaware of the discord as her husband. She went inside to see the children, relieve Marla, and change clothes. Mission accomplished, but she'd keep an eye out just in case.

Dropping the children off to their classes the next morning, Cami went in to see the doctor. Dr. Fleming had been a GP for many years and her doctor for as long as she could remember. It was nice to be greeted and not asked about anything but her past medical history. There was enough recent history to take a few minutes to fill in the gaps. She told him of the two forced penetrations by the man she was now divorced from.

He'd known there was something odd about the way Cami had left so abruptly but professional that he was, he never brought it up. He'd asked her if she had been assaulted, and she declined to answer him in the days before she left. Doc Fleming was the one who confirmed her pregnancy with Eli. He also confirmed that Sawyer hadn't harmed her. She was so horrified that he might think that about Sawyer that she convinced him. He believed her.

"You need to set those children up with me. Good to have a physician that knows some family history. I'll get the receptionist to send you home with forms to fill out. Make them a check-up appointment. Together is fine."

"But she said you weren't taking any new patients. I only got in because you were my doctor previously."

"I'll take care of that. You just do as you're told. Now, Camille, I see you married one of the Knight boys. Is it the one I think it is?"

Camille laughed. "I can't believe you remember that but yes, it is."

"Well, it's about time. That boy's been pining for you for as long as I can remember. That husband of yours hasn't been in for a few years either. He's got a family now. He needs to stay healthy. Work on him for me, will you?"

"I will."

He looked at his computer screen. "Now, let's see what we have here. Well, I hope you like children dear, because it looks like you'll be welcoming another one come about the end of May."

"Really? I'm happy, of course, but the timing is a little sooner than I had wanted. Sawyer will be excited though and at least I'll finish the school year. Right?"

"Or near enough, I imagine." The older man patted her hand. "You'll work it out." He finished setting things up with her, gave her instructions and sent her on her way.

As she was leaving the room he said, "Camille." She looked back. "Glad you're home. Now don't forget the papers at the front desk." She smiled and went to do his bidding before heading to work.

Cami tried to call Sawyer, but it went to voicemail. Out of range was the most likely reason when she couldn't get hold of him during the day. He'd said they needed to do some work, but she didn't remember where. She'd been preoccupied about this appointment. Another try to reach him during lunch produced no better results. It could wait until she got home today. He had thought she was just going to pee in a cup and get the results phoned to her, anyway. She didn't want to tell him she was going to see the doctor.

Having a baby was something she could get excited about after last weekend's conversation. Unlike Aiden, Sawyer wanted their child, but she'd been climbing that mountain in search of happiness for so long, now that she was at the top and settling in to enjoy the view, the vandalism, the parental rejection, the pregnancy, all of it reminded her of how easily it could all turn wrong.

She couldn't shake the feeling that things were still not like she'd dreamed they would be when she and Sawyer were married and raising a family. Camille was determined that would change. No one would take away the happiness they had waited so long to have. She wouldn't let them without the fight of her life.

Marla picked Lily up from school now. It allowed them to not worry about her riding the bus and something happening. When Eli arrived at Cami's office, she put her things away and walked to the car, wondering when they should tell the children another little brother or sister was on its way. Eli wouldn't care as much as Lily. She had been the little princess her whole life. Especially these last months on the ranch.

Cami would have to work on a strategy to help avoid the jealousy. Heaven knew she had enough jealous women surrounding her on any given day to be over her limit. Besides, Lily was all girl and when she found out they could dress the baby up, she'd be all for bringing him or her home. They would have to rearrange the bedrooms but for now, Eli and Lily were still fine together. Sawyer was right though. They needed their own beds. Maybe they'd take care of that this weekend.

She waved goodbye to the office staff and picked up her mail out of her centralized cubby. Tossing the few envelopes and announcement sheets on the front seat, she headed home. When Eli jumped out and raced around the back of the car on his way to greet his Uncle Walker, something stopped his progression.

"Mama. What does M-I-N-E say?"

Cold icy fingers of dread clenched her belly. "What, honey?"

"There're letters on your car. What does M-I-"

"Mine, it spells mine. Go see Uncle Walker, honey. It means the car is Mama's." Eli gave his mother a funny look but shrugged and ran to see Walker.

A bumper sticker on the back of her car proclaimed in huge red letters, 'MINE'. Camille sat on the ground at the back of her car and cried.

Chapter 15

All three Knight brothers were in the chief of police's office alternating between stalking around the room, jabbing their fingers in the air, and demanding in strident tones that something needed to be done. Camille sat quietly in the corner, letting them blow off steam. Better they focus on someone other than her. They had done that for over an hour at the ranch until Piper had come home and said 'enough'.

Camille knew she wasn't hurt physically, but the pain was still there. When would life be normal again? It had been July when she'd decided to return home and try to at least build a relationship with Eli and his father. There had been no more than a few hours in between the finding of that bumper sticker and her news that the baby was confirmed when all hell broke loose.

It was about all she could handle. She had calmed down enough to tell Sawyer the news. That seemed to tip the scale to heading down to the police station. The sheriff was out of town, but his deputy sat in on the meeting. Since the sheriff's department had responded to the Halloween incident, Sawyer thought everyone should be on the same page.

She watched the man she had loved for most of her life and saw the anguish on his face. He was honorable, loved the children, wished the best for others and adored her. Who wouldn't want that type of man? He was someone you could call on in a tight spot and he'd drop everything to help you. All three Knight men would. But when their family was targeted for any type of mischief, all bets were off. The protective men came out in force. No one and nothing was safe from these men if their family was being threatened. It felt good in a terrifying way.

"My wife is pregnant, and this is stress she doesn't need, not to mention the fact that it's harassment and a form of stalking. My attorney," Sawyer turned when the door to the office opened, waving in the direction of the entrance, "is right here."

"Hey, congratulations," said Patrick Daring as he reached his hand out to his friend and client.

He represented all three Knights and shook each man's hand in turn, finishing with a final offered greeting to the chief. Sawyer readily accepted the handshake. A fleeting grin passed his lips at the congratulation before he was serious once again. Patrick was a good attorney and friend. He was also a voice of reason when the Knights lost theirs.

"Sawyer, I understand that you're upset, that you're all upset, but my hands are tied," said the chief.

The deputy was as insensitive in his presentation as he'd been on Halloween night "It's not physically harming anyone and really, it's just a word. That word isn't even threatening."

The chief advised, "All I can say is don't leave her car in the parking lot. The car seems to be the focus of the trouble so remove it from access, at least at school."

The Knights were not happy at the way the conversation was going. Patrick settled things down, gave his opinion and left the room with no doubt that he was watching the results. He did agree with the chief, though. There wasn't anything that could be done at this point but to be vigilant and wait. It would either escalate or go away. Only time would tell.

The men left and after a brief conversation outside the station with Patrick, they went home. "There doesn't seem to be any choice, Cami. I'll drive you to work and pick you back up."

"You can't do that. You have a ranch to run and—"

"A wife to protect. There isn't going to be a discussion on this."

"For how long."

"For as long as it takes to be sure this game someone is playing is over."

Camille wasn't satisfied with the edict, but she felt safer. They dropped Jackson off and picked up the children before heading home. Once there, Camille climbed the stairs, kids in tow.

Walker spoke quietly once he and Sawyer were alone. "I think it's about time we start volunteering at the fire station again."

"Sorry, man, not while all this is going on."

"I think that is exactly why we need to do it. You know we knew what everyone was doing in several counties when we were on the call out sheet. I think it might just be the ticket to figure this mess out. If you cover the weekends, Jack and I will cover the weekdays and respond when we can."

"Damn, that's a good idea. Let's take care of that tomorrow."

One quick phone call to Jackson and then another one to the firehouse and it was set. Almost immediately, they began to get trickles of the goings on around the county. Walker's plan was brilliant, and Sawyer appeared more relaxed now which, in turn, seemed to calm everyone else. Camille was happy that the atmosphere was calmer. True to his word, Sawyer took them to school and he or someone else picked them up.

On the rare occasion he wasn't available, he called and texted to tell her who would be picking her up. When she didn't answer or respond quick enough, he called the office. The first time that happened, Cami answered quickly. He had the principal himself arriving at her office door and waiting until she had spoken to Sawyer before returning to his own work. She kept her cell with her at all times after that.

Christmas break arrived and there was a collective sigh of relief. Nothing else had happened and life was full of Christmas and laughter, not worries of finding that word somewhere. As they were prone to do, the winter holidays were quickly over. School started again, and Camille began to drive to work amid complaints from her husband.

Unfortunately, the area seemed to have a rash of fires and the guys were called out more often. They chatted about the gossip but when they realized Camille had heard some of it, they stopped discussing it in the house. She was just as happy not to hear more than what she was already privy to. The first week, she was apprehensive, worried things would return to the way they were before Christmas, but things went without a hitch. Sawyer, however, had a new issue to complain about.

"Camille, you're doing too much, honey. You're having a baby. You need to slow down and do less."

"Sawyer, stop it. Piper does all sorts of things and she is further along than me by months. I didn't even have you around to help me the last two times. Even when Aiden thought Eli was his, he never helped me out. If it's too heavy, or I'm too tired, I promise to ask for your help but until then, I can handle things."

Sawyer rubbed his hands over the back of his head in frustration. "Cami, I want to be a part of this more than going to the doctor with you once a month."

"You are. You take the children riding after school. That gives me time to relax. I've never had that."

Sawyer wasn't happy and when Jackson laughed at him, he gave him the finger of brotherly love. The gossip had been flying all around during December but come January, things had calmed down. Piper was entering her last month of pregnancy and Camille helped where she could and when she could sneak it past her too vigilant husband.

Camille laughed at a funny story told by another teacher. She dropped mustard onto her shirt as she laughed which made her laugh even more. "Sawyer said I have turned into a klutz with this baby. I wear every meal on my belly instead of putting it in my belly."

The inhabitants of the table in the teachers' lounge where she now took lunch now, erupted with answering laughter. The gossip had ended and most of the teachers spoke to her now. Those who didn't weren't worth the time. That was how she saw it, anyway.

Karl had grown quieter, but it looked like he had a girl-friend now, one of the district employees. Camille was happy he'd found someone to spend time with and since it was one of the women that Walker had told her always hit on Sawyer, she was even more glad. But Karl was a nice guy, and she hoped the woman didn't fixate on him when they called it quits.

Walking back to her nurse's station, Camille stopped at the administration office to pick up her mail. Being a district small enough to house all the schools meant some things were centralized, including lounges and the mailroom. She grabbed her mail, thumbed through it and saw most were flyers of events and general school notices. Opening the plain envelope with no return address, she figured it was an invitation or some such thing. Maybe the receipt for something she had donated to recently.

Inside was a pressed and dried single red rose and the note attached said, 'MINE'. A red rose, and red letters. Indicating love? Dried might have meant a special memory? A long-ago love? What? She felt nauseous. Little boy Knight was probably wiggling around in her belly, having been perked up from lunch. Camille absently placed her hand on her tummy and entered her office, closing the door behind her.

This had gone on long enough. Just when she had relaxed, thinking whoever was angry at her for taking Sawyer from them was over, this started again. Her first instinct was to call Sawyer but really, what good would that do? No, she needed to think about this for a while. Was someone just messing with her mind for no specific reason but that it was a sadistic way to have some fun or was there another reason?

Sawyer had contacted all the women he had dated for more than one time in the past year before she returned home. She had heard of his exploits but really, there were only five. Five women in a year he asked out and none did he ask to his bed. He'd been open with Camille and said he had wanted to find something arousing about them but once he got them in private, it just didn't spark his libido.

"And a man can usually get off on anything given just a little encouragement. It was all your fault," Sawyer declared in mock lament.

Camille had laughed but did he tell anyone he was still carrying a torch for her? Did any of the women feel if he could let go of Camille, then they would have a chance? Had anyone been working on that until she showed up and ended their prospects?

She'd have to ask him again. For now, she'd keep this envelope and its contents a secret. Was it possible that the person doing this was enjoying the uproar over their deliveries? Maybe if she kept it to herself and did not bring in the police, then they would believe no one cared any longer and stop altogether. Or maybe that she didn't receive it, or she threw it away. She didn't want things to escalate, but she'd had enough.

Using the strategy they taught when children were trying to get attention with bad behavior, believing any attention was good attention, she decided to try it her way for a while. Not be less diligent but be less reactive. She tossed the envelope and its contents into the garbage. Thinking she should keep the evidence if she needed to change her strategy again later, she pulled them out of the trash, shoved them in a larger envelope and put a time, date and location on it. Just in case.

The next day things were quiet. She had a doctor's appointment and Sawyer dropped her off at school on doctor days. It was just easier to go home in one car. Dr. Fleming had gotten Sawyer in for a checkup when he accompanied Camille for her first official prenatal visit, citing the need for him to be in perfect health with the growing family he had. Sawyer didn't have a good enough reason to combat the doctor's logic, so he submitted to the exam. When Dr. Fleming declared him to be sound, Sawyer told him it'd been a waste of time.

"Regardless of how you feel about the checkup, we'll meet in another year to waste another hour together."

Sawyer laughed. "I think you and my wife have been conspiring against me, Doc."

"She might have given me some pointers. Now go home and prepare for this next little one to arrive. First let's get Jackson's here and then we will shift focus, yeah?"

"Yeah, sounds good."

Valentine's day was in two weeks and Piper's baby was due in three. Camille's own belly was more pronounced at twenty-two weeks than it had been for the first two children. She was nearly as big as Piper at thirty-seven weeks. She couldn't imagine how big she'd be by the time it was all said and done.

Today Sawyer frowned when Camille told the doctor she felt fine, just a little more tired. "I have stairs to walk up now and two children to chase after, something I didn't have before. And a husband, and family that I want to do things with, an overall larger life I enjoy living. So, it's a tradeoff I'm more than happy to make."

"Okay, then. I'll just put a bug in Sawyer's ear to not let you get overtired but to let you decide when that is... for now, anyway." He spoke to Sawyer but looked at Camille and winked. "I see how it is. Men stick together."

"See you next month."

As had become their habit since their first appointment, they went to a late lunch and then picked up anything they needed in town, before grabbing Eli from school. Camille was starving when she sat down to order and tried not to order more than she could eat. Several people came up and commented on her enlarging belly, just as they had last month.

Carole Dunlap and several other women ignored Camille as they asked Sawyer how his winter was coming along. She knew it was a regional thing to ask and that she could interject in the conversation at any time but the fact that their sole attention was on Sawyer, rankled. Carole asked if she could bring over the final plans when she next visited her mother out at the ranch. Camille had wanted to say no but Sawyer agreed it would be a good idea.

"Great. I'll come over in the morning."

Yeah, you do that when you know I won't be home. Camille wondered if Carole could be the person who was causing all of this trouble. But that last thing, yesterday, a rose seemed odd for a woman to leave... unless you were a landscape designer. And Carole's company had the school landscape contract. She hadn't seen her around campus but that didn't mean she wasn't there. She had to be at some point, just to check on the work, right? Yeah, she'd have to keep a close eye on that woman. Something told Camille things just weren't right.

She almost told Sawyer about the new delivery yesterday, but she decided not to because she hoped to end it soon. Cami knew that if Sawyer found out she had withheld information, he'd dance a paddled tattoo on her butt that would take weeks to fade but she had to try. She wouldn't do something dumb like Piper had and use herself as bait even if she knew how.

Besides, she was something Piper hadn't been at the time, pregnant. She could try to psyche Carole out though. She still marveled at how her being pregnant didn't knock all other interested parties out of the running. Most women would never have considered chasing a man, but had she even had hopes of gaining his attention, the moment he was married and certainly when his wife became pregnant, she'd have backed off so far, she'd have been a distant memory. Evidently that wasn't true in this case.

The next day was Friday, and that was the day Camille made sure she had all her weekly paperwork done in between any student needs. She finished the last file and sent the last email of the week. With a little time left before grabbing Eli and going home, she decided she'd get more water. She wasn't drinking enough according to the doctor.

Camille didn't like water as much as everyone else seemed to. She'd drink tea, coffee, milk, or her favorite pop. She laughed when Sawyer asked her what kind of coke she wanted. He and his brothers all asked the same thing, not realizing what they were saying. It was a regional thing she had gotten out of the habit of since moving away. She tried to remember to be specific. Running into the administration offices to grab some water as it was the closest to her own office, she smiled when she ran into Karl as he finished work in the back room. Reaching behind him, she checked her box before going home.

"I saw you with your lady friend. I'd like to meet her sometime."

"My... Oh, right, Rhonda. She's nice and all but we aren't dating. We're just friends. That's all it is."

"Well, maybe it will become something more. That's how most good relationships start, as friends."

"Yeah, well, I don't think I'll ever be more than her friend and that is just fine with me. Anyway, how's your baby doing?"

She laughed. "Growing like all babies do. Everything is going along just fine. Sawyer is a little too over-protective, but we don't have too many months to go." Camille glanced at the clock. "Gosh, gotta go. Have a great weekend."

Tossing the paperwork from her desk into her inbox to look at on Monday, she grabbed her jacket and her son. Coming home with Eli, Camille needed a little fresh air. She'd been cooped up too much in the last couple of weeks. She was so ready for a weekend but to be honest, a part of her wished she could just stay home. Sawyer would eat that up and make it happen before the words were completely out of her mouth. Maybe she should let Sawyer pamper her a little.

"Hey, what if I go to the stables with you when you have your riding lesson? You and Lily can show me what you've learned."

"Mama, do you want to ride with us?"

"Well, I don't think your little brother wants to be bouncing around in my belly. I will this summer though. I promise."

"Okay." Camille marveled at how easily her children would just accept things at face value. She wished life was always that simple. She also wished that the woman who wanted her husband would just accept he was Camille's.

Changing her clothes into older comfy sweats, her choices were limited these days, she waved as Lily ran to the stables. They had a chance to ride for thirty minutes every day after Eli got home from school. When the weather changed, they would get to go on short trail rides but for now, the breaking pen was where they rode. Camille stayed out of the way normally, but the bright sunshine and the brisk air called to her today. She needed the invigoration being outside gave her.

Lily was done with her ride after twenty minutes and the ranch hand brought her in, helping her to dismount. Running back to Camille, she crossed Eli's path startling Eli's pony. That in turn caused the pony to jerk Eli in the saddle. The little boy tried to hold on, but Camille could see the momentum to the side was too much and Eli would soon find himself unseated. Sawyer had told Camille that it was a dismount the hard way and had laughed when she'd done it at twelve. No one would laugh if her five-year-old kissed the ground in the same way.

Without thinking, she yelled at Lily to get out of the ring.

Advancing on the pony she caught Eli as he tumbled from his mount. His weight and her tenuous hold on him knocked her off balance, and they both fell. Trying to stay away from the pony's hoof as he stepped back, she felt a sharp pain in her hip. Another bruise Sawyer would have a fit about.

Camille heard shouting but her breath was knocked from her. Eli was trying to get out of her arms, but her instincts were to protect him from the hooves. She tried to lay over him as best she could, still dazed herself, putting herself between him and any danger. More shouting and her son wiggled out from under her.

Sawyer was shouting but Camille was concentrating on her breathing. "Don't move, baby. Hold on."

Walker crouched down next to Sawyer and joined his brother in checking her for injuries.

"I'm okay, guys. I fell, that's all. The kids?" Her breath came in quick halted bursts.

"From the pony?" Sawyer's question was shouted in a mixture of irritation and fear.

"No, I wouldn't ride while I'm pregnant." Now it was her turn to be indignant.

Sawyer sighed. "Thank God. All good then. I sent the kids inside."

"I fell when I caught Eli and it knocked the breath out of me but I'm good now. I just need to let everything settle again."

"Here, honey, let us carry you." Sawyer looked at his brother. "Two-man lift should work. That way we won't hurt her."

"Don't be ridiculous. Just help me stand and get my bearings."

Instead of arguing, the men did what she asked and soon they were helping her walk inside. Her back hurt and her side but otherwise, by dinner, she seemed okay. Camille spent the rest of the evening assuring everyone she had weathered the incident with no ill effects.

"What the hell were you doing in that pen, anyway?"

"Sawyer, stop. I was fine watching until Lily ran to me and spooked Eli's pony. The hand was tying her pony to the rail and didn't see Eli begin to slide off his saddle. I wanted to save him the fall. I'm not going to apologize for it."

"Cami, you're pregnant and have no business in the pen with large animals right now."

"I wanted to watch them ride. I don't do as much with the children these days and I needed to get some fresh air. It was a good idea and I would do it again."

"I'm firing that hand first thing in the morning."

"Sawyer Knight, it wasn't his fault. Lily wanted to finish early, and he did the right thing by tying the pony up. No one could have predicted Lily would have raced past Eli like she did."

"I can't have things like this happen again." Sawyer could be mulish if he had his mind set on things.

"Don't you dare fire him, or I'll rehire him."

Walker sauntered into the room. "You two need to settle down. The kids can hear you." He looked at Cami with his big brother sternness. "Now, I agree with Sawyer. You cannot go in the stables if the horses are out nor a pen when one is in there. We will make sure there is one hand for each kid when they are riding but you will be outside the ring." He turned to his brother. "And that is a good hand. We are not firing him. Camille is right. He did what he needed to do and couldn't have predicted little Miss Piccadilly's actions." Walker stretched out in the leather recliner. "Now, what's on TV?"

Chapter 16

Camille told those at her lunch table Monday about the Friday evening incident. Several of the women who had become closer to Cami talked about the risk. The superintendent walked in to grab his lunch from the fridge and Karl came in behind him.

"I've got a bunch of last year's seeds from Carole Dunlap here." Mr. Watkins placed the bag on the counter. "They're in plastic bags, labeled. If anyone is interested, grab some." He turned to Camille. "So you had a run in with a horse?"

"Not exactly." Cami relayed the highlights to Mr. Watkins. "Sounds like Sawyer is right to limit your activities." He nodded in the direction of her small, rounded belly before he left. Karl was following right behind him but stopped briefly as he passed Camille.

He seemed concerned. "I'm glad you're all right." He hesitated before asking, "You are, aren't you?"

She smiled. "Of course. Thanks for asking." He nodded and left to catch up with his boss. Nice guy. Hope he found a real girlfriend soon.

When she returned from lunch, Cami's smile disappeared.

Damn, another one already? She reminded herself that you expect children's behavior to escalate before it disappears so that's probably what this is. She couldn't help but sigh in frustration when, on her desk, were red flower petals, and a typed note, in large red letters, that read 'MINE'.

Filing it away as she had the previous one, she went on about her day. Becoming a stay-at-home mom was looking better and better these days.

Tuesday, she bumped into the edge of a desk in the elementary office and moaned when she saw the red mark. Several people remarked on it and she could see the beginnings of a rather large circular bruise on her arm. She reassured those who enquired what had happened and unfortunately, she bruised more these days because of the increased blood flow. She was a nurse after all and knew what caused it. Nothing other pregnant women weren't dealing with every day. She hoped no one thought something more sinister was going on. She couldn't deal with another round of gossip.

On Wednesday, there were red petals at her car door on the ground. Just a few and a paper rolled in her door handle that read 'MINE'. She almost didn't read the papers anymore because they never changed. What was she going to do? Either the woman, whoever she was, would end this soon, or it was about to come to a head in the opposite direction. She prayed that wouldn't happen. Not with her carrying around her baby bump.

On Friday, she got chocolates in a heart-shaped dish in her box, but it was close to Valentine's day. Maybe it was from Sawyer. And no note. Definitely from her husband. She smiled and nibbled on the high sugar treat that seemed to relax her. Her work nearly done for the week, she saw a particularly enticing chocolate on the bottom. She reached in the dish to grab it and felt paper. Her hand froze as she processed what that could mean. It really only could mean one thing, but she had to peek to make sure.

Taped to the inside bottom of the dish was a small paper with red letters. 'Mine'.

It was too much. She called Sawyer.

"Sawyer, can you come and get me?"

"Yes." He was moving, she could tell by the sounds on the phone. "What's wrong, baby? Do we need to go to the hospital? Should I call an ambulance?"

"No," she heard the whine and tears that caused her voice to waiver. She sniffed. She might have cared before but not now. All she wanted was to feel safe.

"Can you pick me up from my office?"

"You're sure?"

She sniffed again. "I'm sure."

"Okay, sweetheart, I'll be there soon. I'm already pulling out of the drive."

"Thank you."

She hung up because she wanted him to concentrate on the road, not her. Suddenly she was too tired to do anything alone. Her emotions were heightened, and all she wanted to do was go home and go to bed leaving everything with Sawyer to handle. Staying in the building was too much now that she knew he was on his way. She wanted to meet him in the parking lot. She signed out on the computer and told the office she was going home.

"Not feeling that good. I'll see you Monday."

She slowly walked through the hallway and out the front doors of the administration offices. When she looked up, she sighed her relief. Her Knight in shining armor was pulling into the parking lot. He must have broken all the speed limits to get here so soon. She sat on the steps and waited for him to come to her. The concern on his face as he rocketed out of the driver's door said it all. Tears streamed down her face as she watched him jog to her. Without one word, he tucked her hair behind her ears and kissed her. Right on the front steps. And she kissed him back.

"Come on, baby, let's get you home."

She nodded and with Sawyer's strong steady arms around her, she stood and leaned on him as they walked to the truck. He helped her inside and kissed her again before buckling her in and shutting the door. The sight of him trying to see over her belly to connect the seatbelt made her laugh, and that was what she needed. Sawyer to make her feel better.

"I love you."

"I adore you."

The door shut and in no time at all they were pulling in at the ranch.

"Let's get you inside, baby. Take a nap and you'll feel better."

"I'd like that but Sawyer, I need to talk to you about things."

"Life and death things?"

"No."

"Okay, then take a nap and we can talk afterwards. I'll be in the office downstairs. Call if you need me."

"Sawyer, you can finish your work."

"Nope. Lily is tired too, so I'll bring her up to you and she can nap beside you."

"I'd like that almost as much as napping with you. But not quite."

Sawyer seemed to consider something but shook his head with a grin. "You need to rest and napping with me won't do that for you." Cami smiled.

After dinner, Piper and Jackson came over. "I'm restless. This baby is due any day and I'm ready to have her."

The women chatted inside as the two brothers went outside to walk the ranch as it relaxed them during the winter night. "Something isn't right. She's gone quiet this last couple of weeks but Cami has gotten more off-balance and I don't mean like when she fell catching Eli."

"I understand off-centered. Piper is so close to delivery, she's well off her mark which makes her madder than a wet hen in the snow with alligator teeth."

"Yeah, scary stuff. She wants to talk but I think we will cover what's going on with her tomorrow, after a full night's sleep. You, on the other hand, will have to just wait for a baby."

Jackson huffed a resigned laugh. "Yeah, but at least my end is in sight. You have months." Sawyer groaned.

"Heard any more on the crazy woman?"

"No, and that bugs me. You know?"

"Hey, don't complain. I think it's good. Don't go trying to figure out why, just be glad."

"You thought any more about Camille staying home?"

Sawyer shut the barn door. "Every day and on days like today, I wanted to just say she had to tender her resignation and stay home, but that isn't who we are together even if it's how I feel. It won't work if she doesn't agree, but I gotta tell ya, I was so close today I had to bite my tongue."

"I think she's coming around to your way of thinking. It won't be long now."

Sawyer sat back in his chair in the office and sipped the smooth scotch, contemplating life. Camille was more skittish tonight, and that didn't change with Piper and Jackson coming around. It might have been because she'd had a bad day, or because she wanted to talk and they had visitors instead. He wondered if she was still thinking of finishing the school year. They had three more months to go. He couldn't imagine her working with everything else going on but as she pointed out to him every time he asked if she wanted to stay home, she'd done this and more before coming back.

Dammit, he knew she had and could again if necessary but it wasn't. It was a team effort and right now, she was putting herself and their baby at risk, not to mention Eli and Lily needed their mom. He knew it was a low blow to bring that up with her but he was worried and he wanted to bring his family in tight, closing the surrounding access. Old rancher style.

What was more concerning is that she had wanted to tell him something, and by her behavior tonight, it was bothering her she hadn't told him earlier. That was on him. He hadn't let her, pushing her to sleep, She'd needed it. He worried that what she was going to tell him he didn't want to hear.

Monday was Valentine's day, a commercial holiday for sure but one he wanted to exploit this year. Since she left home and him, she'd not had a Valentine's day. Not had anyone to pamper her or take care of her. That was unacceptable.

Now, what to do? Flowers? Only if they were planted afterwards. A single rose? That sounded more their style. She wouldn't complain about wasting money on cut flowers that died quickly if it was just one. He'd still get to say he loved her. Chocolate? The darker the better.

Since she had stopped feeling queasy, chocolate had become her friend. Now the card wouldn't be easy. Maybe he'd let the kids each grab her one or better yet, make her one. The library was having a special children's afternoon tomorrow for a couple hours for just that project. He must not be the only dad with planning and creative issues. And he loved he had those problems.

Life had become so complicated and so simple at the same time. Gaining a family he'd wanted for so long without actually talking about it, made things simple. But in the same breath, meals, working, relaxation, hell, even thinking became more complicated now with so many other people's needs to put before his. This time last year, the most complicated thing he had to worry about was whether he'd spend the night in or go out and whether buying that four-wheeler was a good idea or not.

Now life was more than good, it was incredible. The nucleus of his love was complicated, to be sure, but right now, she was waiting for him to crawl in bed with her. And he'd be dammed if he made either of them wait any longer. The rest would be figured out tomorrow or the next day because he had the life where there was another day.

Saturday came sunny and frosty. He had things in town that needed to get done, the kids needed to make those valentines this afternoon, and Sawyer needed to convince his girl to take it easy. She woke up achy and cranky. He had some chores to do, and he left early to get them done. He had plenty of hands to do the work but some things he liked doing on his own. Feeding his own horse and now the kids' ponies were on that list. Eli enjoyed helping but little Miss Princess Lily didn't care to get her hands dirty, opting to stay on the porch and inside the house.

He got out before anyone else was up and that suited him fine. Chores were quicker that way. Finishing his instructions for the day, not that he needed to tell them much because their foreman was better than most, it was time for breakfast and his conversation with his wife. Whatever she had to say, he wanted it out of the way before dinner so he'd have time to work on a solution if one was needed.

Chapter 17

Plopping back in bed before taking his shower, Sawyer kissed Cami. "Morning, beautiful."

She groaned. "I'm not beautiful, I'm fat, ugly, tired, and grumpy. You should run while you still can."

Laughing, Sawyer reached down, bringing her face to his, he kissed her deeper. "I love you that way."

"Liar."

"I haven't paddled your butt in months. I think I still can if I'm careful or maybe I can do more creative punishments. I heard they are very effective for naughty pregnant wives."

"You wouldn't."

He raised his eyebrow. "Unless you are desperate to test the theory, sweetheart, I wouldn't call me out."

"Fine." She pushed him away. "I have to get up and get the kids dressed. Have they eaten?"

"Don't know but they've figured out more complicated things than getting cereal. If not, they know how to ask. That's if they're even up." His manner became more serious as he sat further on the bed, leaning back against the headboard. "I need to talk to you or rather I think you need to talk to me. Now is as good a time as any with your grumpy self on display." He tucked her hair around her ear. "What happened yesterday?"

His girl shut down right before his eyes. "I had a hard day. That's all. Hormones."

"Nice try, baby, but Daddy asked a question, and he needs a straight answer."

And that was all it took. Damn, he'd have to remember that as he watched his wife crawl into his lap. "Sawyer, I meant to tell you but you said we could talk later and I was tired, then we had dinner, and then—"

He dropped his voice naturally but enjoyed her reaction.

"Camille Constance Knight, do not test me."

She sighed. "Remember when I said things were quiet at work? Nothing out of the ordinary going on?"

"Yes." He made sure his tone was not encouraging.

"I wasn't exactly truthful."

Sawyer didn't mean to jolt her as much as he did when he sat up. He grabbed his girl as she began to scramble out of his lap. "Stop, baby. What has been going on?"

He tried to gentle his tone, but it was with herculean effort. They had gone through short stretches of time when things were quiet with their crazy lady, but now he knew it might not have been as quiet as he'd thought.

Cami began to sniffle, and he had to stave this off. If she started to cry, it would be a good hour before he got the whole story and he needed it sooner not later.

"Cami, Daddy is waiting."

"Fine. All right." She sniffed indignantly. He almost smiled. She was adorable, his little brat. She hadn't told him things she should and now when she was called on it, she had the pluck to be indignant. Lily would be a handful if she took after her mother.

"Well, remember when I said nothing was happening?" This time when she paused he didn't respond. "I've been getting things like rose petals, a rose, notes, you know, stuff like that. Yesterday, I got chocolates in a heart dish I thought was from you but at the bottom of the dish was a note with the same word in red."

"How many?" he asked through clenched teeth.

"Three this week."

"Three? What the..."

She rushed on to explain. "I was trying to see if I didn't respond or have anyone show up like the police, you know, pretend it wasn't a big deal, then they would quit."

"Camille, three times in one week? That is the opposite of ignoring."

"I know, I know, but it's like children. When you ignore certain behaviors, they escalate and then the behavior extinguishes."

"Evidently not."

"But it might still be in the escalation stage."

"Cami, baby, do you hear yourself? You are more vulnerable than normal being six months pregnant." He saw the tears begin to roll down her cheeks, and he wanted to kick his own ass but still, it wasn't something she could keep to herself. "How am I going to keep you safe if I don't even know what I'm battling? You need to tell me when things happen. I think you should go on leave or something until this mess stops."

"I can't."

"Well, I'm done messing around now. I'm putting an end to this."

"Sawyer, what are you talking about? How are you going to do that?"

"Draw them out."

"Right, like that worked so well for Piper." Cami sighed. "I know this is hard for you. You want to be the big bad protector but sometimes we don't have control. I know you're frustrated."

"And now I'm going on the offense. I'm done waiting for something to happen to you. For her to do something to give herself away."

Camille asked him hesitantly, "It's not Carole, right?"

"I don't really see how but everyone is a suspect in my mind and I mean everyone."

"What does that mean?"

Sawyer pulled her close kissing the top of her head. "Nothing really. It's just, I'm so frustrated. It has to be someone that has access to the school and just about everyone does."

"Yes, but these were in my school inbox."

He stiffened. "Who has access to that?"

"Employees in the school system. I guess, if you are in the office and no one is paying attention, and know what that the cubbies are there and..."

"Well, that narrows it down but not by much."

"Okay, but since it's a woman who has either dated you, wanted to date you, or at least dreamed of dating you, and not a man... Well, unless he's gay but since you aren't, not male. So, no one in maintenance, and that knocks about fifteen people off the list."

"Leaving how many?"

Cami rolled her eyes to the ceiling then looked at her fingers as they moved in some type of counting method. She grinned.

"Less than fifty in the school. Unless they were people off the street. Every woman has the hots for the Knight men."

"Cami, you are exaggerating. I can work with that school number. How did you figure that out?"

"I have to make sure everyone is up on their physicals and their immunizations."

"Good thinking for a naughty girl who will soon find herself paying penance for her penchant for keeping secrets and lying to her daddy."

"Sawyer, see this big basketball right here? My get out of jail free card, among other things. I'm pleading hormonal insanity."

"I'll just keep track and we will meet up after number three has made an appearance."

"You'll have forgiven me by then."

"I forgive you already but I'll always want to beat your ass just a little."

"If it didn't get me so hot and bothered, I'd say you were a pervert."

"And you'd be right. Up, baby. I have things to do today. You have nothing to do but rest."

"No punitive punishment?"

"Nope. I'm saving it up for when I can really light up your world. Now, I'm jumping in the shower, grabbing the munchkins and heading into town. You are not to leave this ranch. Not the house would be even better but front porch is fine if you can handle the chilly weather out there today."

"Mm-kay."

He smiled when she was asleep again by the time he'd showered and left the bedroom. His day had suddenly gotten fuller. He'd have to wait ongoing to the police station until the afternoon when he could drop off the kids at the library. Until then, he'd get the rest of his errands done. For a split second, he missed not being able to just jump in his truck and go but he gained so much for that loss of freedom.

"Daddy, I don't think I should have to use this car seat if Eli doesn't."

"Well, you do and you see more from there because you sit higher."

"Oh." And that was the end of Lily's complaint. He was getting better at parenting.

By the time he picked the children up and was on his way home, him with his gifts, them with theirs, everyone was tired and hungry. The weekends were every man for himself because he had given Belinda off until Tuesday. It made it easier because that woman, even though she had said she understood Cami and the situation, never warmed up totally to her. It made weekends easier if she were able to go to her daughter's or sisters'.

He thought about grabbing burgers but Cami would skin him alive for getting what she called junk food when it wasn't a special occasion. She would make them at home but with healthy sides. No chips. No carbonation, no extra sugary baked beans from a can and so on. Anything he could throw together in twenty minutes was usually frowned upon. So, hitting one of the few fast-food places for dinner put her into her mama-mode.

Shaking his head at how he had changed, he grabbed pork chops, Cami's favorite, and headed home. He got frozen lasagna for tomorrow and steak for Monday, Valentine's Day. It was his favorite food but he could cook beef better than anything else. Cami said it was a guy thing, he preferred to think it was a rancher thing.

As they walked to the truck, he couldn't believe what he saw. 'MINE' blazed across the tailgate of his pickup. He hadn't thought and parked against the grouping of trees at the corner of the small grocery store lot. Anyone could have gotten in there and spray painted the word without being noticed.

As he drove home ignoring the cranky children in the back seat, Sawyer wondered how he'd flush the woman out without putting his wife in danger or anyone else. Pulling into the ranch, he decided the way to bring out the woman who thought he was her property was to make her think he was looking for some entertainment on the side. He didn't know how he'd do that without making his real woman upset but he had to work on it.

After telling Cami how he found his truck decorated, he promised he'd find a way to settle this. He put in a conference call to Jackson who couldn't leave Piper. She was showing signs of going into labor at any moment. He roped in Walker who was in Austin convincing Josie to take a job closer to him and the ranch. He talked to his closest friend, his brothers, to discuss his plan before he laid it out for Cami.

"Camille can't deal with this much longer," said Sawyer after relaying to his brothers the events of the week that until today, had been undisclosed.

"Why is it that these women think they can handle things on their own?" asked Jackson.

"Camille and I have had a talk about that."

"Let me know if it works. I'll try your methods myself," said Jackson.

Walker stayed silent. Sawyer continued, "I figure if I go to the Whet Whistle, act friendly like, it might trigger something we could hang our hat on. At the rate we're going, we'll all be old and gray before we figure out who she is."

Sawyer could hear Walker's tone and knew his brother was shaking his head. "Seems to me that there isn't anything that could cause a whole town to come unglued except if you looked like you were trolling right after you married Camille and settle your baby in her belly. I know I'd be looking for a back alley with your name on it."

"Never mind the babies you already have." Jackson was skeptical. "I don't think you'd better try that. Besides, it would open Camille up for all kinds of new ridicule."

"I don't have another choice. There isn't anything else to do."

"You sound like Piper," cautioned Jackson. "And I promise, in this type of situation, that isn't good."

"I'll think about it more, but you guys have to promise to have my back. I'll talk to Camille and if she's against it, I'll drop it."

"WHAT ARE YOU SUGGESTING you do? Encourage women to think you are available?"

"Not available, but maybe I have a wandering eye, enough so we can draw this crazy woman out."

"No. I mean, Sawyer, what if they follow you home? Or, I don't know, take you up on your flirting?"

"Honey, men flirt. That's what they do but when you came back to town, even before then, I hadn't done more than a little innocent flirting and no matter how many women offered me all sorts of attractions, I usually turned it down. We'd dance, sit with others, drink a little, but I rarely took them up on their availability. I'd leave 'em at the door."

"So you were the male version of a cock tease. Great. No wonder someone is after you and had taken possession of you in her mind. You represent the one who got away from everyone."

He reached to draw her closer to him. She needed the comfort, and he needed the connection. "I wouldn't have thought so. I was always honest and up front. Most guys are in for a good time before they dump the girl but I didn't do that unless they demonstrated they understood me."

"I know and I'm not blaming you. I've stopped blaming myself for ever leaving. That was another place and time. I was young and easily influenced. I thought people were truthful and all other options were closed to me. But now, I want to fight this. I'm tired of being a victim and tired of waiting for someone else to make the next move. I understand why Piper did what she did, now. It's frustrating."

He kissed the top of Cami's head and pulled her back to sit in the cradle of his thighs and forged ahead. "I think I'll do something similar but less dangerous."

"You're serious? You are talking out of frustration but real contemplation? You want to bait the crazy woman?"

Her body tensed and he had expected that reaction. He rubbed her arms soothingly and kissed her cheek. Resting his chin on the top of her fragrant hair, turning her to face him, Sawyer kissed her nose and made his point.

"Hear me out. I think if I go into the Whet Whistle and hang out, as though I needed a break from the house, it will draw that person out fast. I mean, you'd think they would want to make contact, right?"

"And make everyone in town think we're already tired of each other or at least you're tired of us?"

"I know that might be a side effect until we have this person caught but, honey, we can't go on like this. It has gone on for months and that is more energy than we should have put into something so destructive to our happiness." Camille sagged against him. "I know."

They sat, Camille enclosed in Sawyer's arms and legs, he worrying about what she was thinking. "I think you should try it."

He hesitated worried there was a 'but' somewhere in that sentence. "You sure?"

"Yup. Go tonight if you want. It's only eight and a weekend night. I'm kind of tired and I won't have to sit here worrying about it all. I'll sleep through it."

Sawyer took a deep breath and let it out in resignation and a touch of excitement that maybe they would be done with all of this soon. "Okay, I agree. I gotta change shirts so I look the part but then let's see if this draws the monster out."

"Should I be worried you seem to be overly jubilant to play the male floosy to expose some crazy person?"

"Nope, excited. We might be through with this in just a couple of days." He dropped a kiss on her lips and was soon heading out the door with a clean western shirt on and his good Stetson.

It was after two a.m. before Sawyer dragged his tired ass in the door. It had been the most surreal night he'd ever had. Women were coming out of the woodwork. Some frowned at him and left him alone. Some, he knew, were already passing the gossip ten minutes after he arrived alone. And then there were the ones who didn't worry about sharing him or lecturing him. Those were the ones he focused on. It was possible one of those overanxious females was the stalker.

By the end of the evening, he had a pounding headache, a dick that had withdrawn into his pelvis trying to retreat from the blatantly obvious come-ons, and a stomach sick from guilt at trying this shit in the first place. He prayed it did what he wanted it to and not just caused more trouble. Time would tell.

He jumped in the shower downstairs before heading up to his girl. He wouldn't upset her by coming in smelling like a tomcat on the prowl. Even though he had played that part tonight. Camille snuggled into him as he crawled in next to her. He had no idea how he rated such a beautiful woman as Cami but he wouldn't risk losing her to some crazy chick with rejection issues.

Chapter 18

Camille heard Sawyer come in the kitchen door and relaxed. She'd dozed all night since he'd left and didn't realize she was listening for him until he got home. Safe and sound and back in her bed. She thought she was secure in who they were but those years away put some doubt and worry in the once youthful relationship and now gave her concern where none existed before. She did her best to ignore the creeping doubts.

It was a warm and clear Sunday. In the late afternoon, Jackson called to check on Sawyer and to say they might have a baby in the next day or two. Cami went over to check on how her sister-in-law was doing and confirmed she was looking done. "I'm pretty sure you're having all the signs of motherhood within the next twenty-four hours."

"You think? I hope so. I'm so done with being pregnant. We're ready for the next stage of our lives."

"I remember that feeling with both of mine for different reasons. We are so ready for your little one but we're not ready for our next little Knight to be here. I have things I'm trying to finish before I'll be ready. But you look and sound miserable. I'd say that means let's have a baby."

"Every so often there is a ripple across my pelvis but nothing really more than that."

"Getting ready. Have you thought of the name, for real?"

"Yeah, we have agreed on Janine Aurora Knight. Janine was my mom's name. Aurora because I love it and because if we put an 'A' name in the middle her initials spell JAK. Like her daddy, Jackson-JAK."

"I love it! You're positive it's a girl?"

"Yep, no question, apparently. I'm ready and so is Jackson. It's time to have her and settle in for the changes."

"Yeah, I remember that time but it was stressful for me with the first two. This one has a different stress."

"I know. Jackson told me Sawyer was thinking of trying to lure this woman out by creating doubt in her mind that you two were still happy."

Camille sighed. "I know. He went to the Whet Whistle last night."

"I thought he was just thinking about it."

"Nope. He isn't one to wait around once he decides on a course of action."

"But what about you?"

"We talked about it and I agreed because I'm just as tired of dealing with this as he is. I'd thought they would give up but just last week they got more intense. It was hard, but I let him go out."

"And?"

"Well, we don't know, do we? It's only been about twelve hours since he got home. Which reminds me, tell Jackson to come over and eat with us while you are in the hospital if he leaves you at all while you two are there."

Piper laughed as she waved Camille out. "I'll tell him but don't look for him."

"I won't."

After the kids went to sleep, Sawyer sat with Camille in bed.

"Sawyer, I'm going to work."

"Stay home tomorrow. Just one day."

"I went home early on Friday."

"Two hours early. I'm worried about you going tomorrow."

"Sawyer, I can't just stop working because a stupid woman with issues is trying to cause trouble."

"Fine, then you call me every hour."

Camille laughed. "I know you're worried but I'm not calling you every hour. You aren't even available to take my call every hour."

"Camille, I love you but the bottom line is I'm your husband and if I think it's the right thing to do, you'll do it." Cami rolled her eyes.

"Don't push your luck, Casanova."

"Dammit, why won't you let me take care of you?"

"I am but you are being unreasonable."

Things were quiet. Finally, Sawyer said, "Then when you get there, at lunch, and when you are in the car, about to come home you call. Those are only three times."

"That I can do."

"I wish you'd stop fighting me."

Camille could feel the heaviness of her heart weighing on her. The tears slid slowly down her cheeks. "I don't want to fight with you, Sawyer. It makes me sad and tired." She cuddled into his arms. "I'm weary of this whole thing. I just want to stay home and enjoy my life and my family."

"You mean it? I don't want you to lose your skills but I'm ready for you to be home whenever you are."

"I mean it. Let me try to last a little longer. Closer to my due date if I can."

"I can back off and let you do that. For now. But if things get worse, you are calling it quits sooner."

"Okay."

"Okay. But tomorrow. I'm worried about this whole thing and it being Valentine's Day, you know? It's just one more day, honey. You need this break and it will make me feel better."

"If you promise it's just one more day."

"Promise."

THE CALL CAME IN AT seven a.m. "Piper has gone into labor and we are our way to the hospital. I'll call when we have another Knight here safe and sound."

"You need anything? You want me to cover for you at the ranch?"

"Nope we have things covered. I called her office."

"Jackson, do you need me to come?" Cami asked into the phone.

"Thanks, Camille but we want to do this ourselves."

"Of course. Lots of love. See you both soon."

Camille called and gave Marla the day off because she was home and could pick up Lily. The house phone rang again at eleven-thirty, just before Sawyer left to pick Lily up from preschool.

"Walker, it's all hands-on deck. Seems like a brush fire has started out by the old Carriage place."

"That's at the edge of our area isn't it? Nothing but fields for a few miles or more."

"I know, but then there is the Proctor farm on the other side of that and they have plenty to lose. It'll burn fast so we need to get a rush on it."

Sawyer looked at Camille and dropped a hard hurried kiss on her lips. "Sorry, baby, but I have to go help on this one. Can you pick up Lily and come straight back home?"

"Yep. You two stay safe and do what you can. We'll be here when you get back." Kissing her again, Sawyer grabbed his gear from the mud room and headed out the door.

Camille arrived a few minutes before school was released for Lily so she ran into her office to check her phone messages. She placed her own phone on vibrate as was her habit in the school. She pressed the messages button on her desk phone and sat back to listen. There were a few information ones and parents returning her calls. The last one was from the administration office asking her to call when she got the message. She redialed the number and Karl answered.

"Hey, you missed the message on Friday afternoon that Lily's class was taking an extra half hour to finish their Valentine's project today. They'll be done at twelve-thirty instead of twelve."

"Oh, well that's okay. I'll just finish listening to my voicemails after I run to the bathroom." She laughed. "Side effect of pregnancy. Thanks for letting me know."

"Welcome."

Camille couldn't believe how many times she had gone to the bathroom today. She wondered how Jackson and Piper were doing. She sent a text but didn't call in case they were in the middle of something important. The response was fast.

Camille: How are things? My niece here yet?

Jackson: Piper's in transition.

Camille: Woot! Won't be long now.

Jackson: Yep. Gotta go.

Camille's smile grew as she slid the phone into her front pocket. She'd sat on it enough during this pregnancy. She'd break it if she wasn't careful. Sawyer would pitch a fit if he couldn't find her when he thought he needed to talk to her. She never realized how needy men were until recently. She hadn't felt this wanted and loved in years, so it was a good trade off. Opening her door to the first aid room, she wondered what she should do for another twenty minutes.

The whole room looked like it had puked roses and rose petals. They were literally everywhere she looked. They were on her desk, the windowsill, the floor, her chair, everywhere. Her thoughts froze for a second and then the overwhelming urge to escape pushed through her mind. Run, her brain screamed. There was a shuffling sound behind her. Fear mixed with relief that someone was with her pushed through her panic.

"Hel–"

A hand was over her mouth pressing hard, and a sting followed what felt like a needle prick on the side of her neck. Injection. Someone was injecting her with some kind of drug. Nausea, dizziness.

"WHO THE HELL WOULD call in a fire when there wasn't one? In this remote corner?" asked Sawyer as they turned the truck around to head home.

"Don't know, man. In the movies, it would be to get the hero off the scent of the villain," said Walker. "Wonder if we are uncles?"

"Let me call Camille to see if she has heard anything." He hit her recall number and wondered why she didn't pick up. The phone rang as soon as he left a message. "Hey, baby."

"Yeah, you need to cut that shit out. I do have a baby though. She's here."

"Sorry, thought you were Camille. Congrats on our little niece." The guys congratulated their brother, hooted and hollered a bit before saying they would come by before going home.

"Hey, is Camille with you?" asked Jackson.

"No, why?"

"She texted us about half an hour ago and we were close. But I've called and texted her with the news with no response."

"She might be on her way home after picking up Lily," offered Sawyer but he didn't like the way his stomach clenched.

"Maybe. Let me know, will you? I have a funny feeling."

"Me too, now. Take care of Piper and the baby. I'll call back as soon as I talk to her."

"Thanks, man."

Sawyer sat silent for a few minutes and tried to call Camille again with only voicemail as a response. Sawyer called the house while Walker called Cody Race, their foreman. No luck. Walker watched Sawyer change directions. "School?"

"Yep," was Sawyer's tight-lipped response.

Sawyer's phone rang again. "Hello?"

"Mr. Knight?"

"Yes."

"Lily hasn't been picked up from school and she's been here waiting for over half an hour. We thought someone was just running late, but..."

"I'm on my way there now." Sawyer turned to Walker. "Have you checked my wife's office?"

"No, she called in sick this morning so it never occurred to me that she might be in the building."

"Could you do that for me? I'm on the way there."

Sawyer looked over at Walker. "The school is checking her office but Cami hasn't picked up Lily yet. Something has happened. Can you call Cody and see if his wife can come grab Lily from us?"

"Got it. What do you think has happened to her?" Walker asked as he dialed their foreman.

"Nothing good."

Cody and his wife Marilyn met them at the school. She took Lily and after they found Camille's car but no Camille, she took Eli home too. He wasn't happy but Sawyer's grim face quieted him quickly.

"What the hell has happened?" asked Sawyer.

"Don't know. Let's not panic. Maybe she fell asleep in her office?"

"Yes, that could have happened," said Sawyer although neither of them believed it. "The office worker said no one was in the office but the door was unlocked and the light was on."

"Is that common during a school day?" asked Cody as Marilyn got the children buckled in the seat.

"I don't think so. She said the first aid room was only accessible from her office so she tried to lock the main door when she wasn't in it."

As they approached her office, they could see a sliver of light shining under the door but the knob was locked in place. That was odd because she was a stickler for turning lights out after leaving a room and they had just told him the door was unlocked.

They went to the superintendent's office. "Mr. Watson, have you seen Camille?"

"No, I thought she had lost track of time when the elementary called looking for her. I told them she was off today and they said she wasn't answering her phone. When my wife was pregnant, she was tired all the time. I wondered if she'd fallen asleep."

Sawyer was irritable. "Her car is outside, and I left her to go to a bogus fire while she came to get Lily. Now we can't find her after she obviously arrived. Where else could she be?" The desperation was making his delivery of the questions almost violent.

"Carole Dunlap. Has she been here today?" demanded Walker.

"Ms. Dunlap? Yes. Just before lunch I think. Why?"

Sawyer slammed his hand down on the counter. "Cami thought she might have been the one doing all this 'MINE' crap. Looks like she's right."

Walker clamped his hand on Sawyer's shoulder. Hard. "Hold on. Slow down and let's think."

Sawyer kept talking. "She works with flowers, her mother said she'd be better for me. She's always around and ignores Camille."

"I don't think it could have been her. Her truck is gone. She left right after talking to Karl," said Mr. Watson.

"Maybe," said Sawyer. "But I'm going to need proof."

Walker asked. "Where else could she be? Can we ask for her on the intercom?"

Mr. Watson brightened. "Yes, we could." He turned to the desk in front of his office and frowned. "Karl is usually here to do these sorts of things. I wonder where he's gone off to?"

Sawyer almost choked the school superintendent. "Can we get a key to her office?"

"Of course. Karl has all the spares on a big ring in his desk somewhere."

They dug through the desk with no luck. Mr. Watson was perplexed. Walker opened the last drawer and pulled things out.

Rose petals. He looked at Sawyer. "Hey, didn't you say one of those times last week there was rose petals? These aren't real but..." He shrugged.

"Yes, yes. It could be nothing but we need to find him," said Sawyer.

Mr. Watson explained. "But he's Camille's friend. Kind of looked out for her in the early weeks of the crazies."

"Get maintenance, Mr. Watson. We are breaking into the nurse's office. It's Karl. Call the police station and let them know it wasn't about me, it was about Camille all along. It was Karl claiming Camille and warning me off, not the other way around. It makes sense now. Shit. He's missing and so is she. Let's go."

Chapter 19

The door to Camille's office was opened partly by maintenance, and when the Knight men were too impatient, a few kicks to the wood. It flew open and the force of the movement swirled a breeze that gave the room a snow globe effect. A snow globe filled with rose petals and roses. Camille's purse was still on the desk. Without a phone.

The police arrived and took her phone number, the chief making a few calls and declaring they would find where her phone was pinging if it was still on.

"Wait, I have a tracking device on my phone. We loaded it when we found out she was pregnant. She said so she could find me."

The huff of incredulity Sawyer released might have tried to mimic a laugh, but it failed miserably sounding more like a groan of desperation from a man looking for his woman, in fear for her safety.

"Here. It says she is here in the building."

Mr. Watson spoke up. "School will be out in forty-five minutes. Then it will be bedlam if I don't get control now." The chief, who had come when he found out who was missing, said he'd help the superintendent. They would coordinate the orderly removal of the children.

"Sawyer, fire training. Systematic clearing of rooms. Standard plan except looking only for Cami."

Mr. Watson looked over at Sawyer and Walker. "Don't worry about us and the kids, just find Camille."

Walker and several officers made a plan of action, stopping Sawyer just before he opened every door in the hall. "Sawyer, we're splitting up and going by twos. You're with me. We have this area to clear before checking in."

"Right. You take that room. I'll take this one. It's faster."

"We do it together, it's safer."

"Fuck safety. My pregnant wife is being held by a man who believes she belongs to him like his property. We get her to safety."

Walker's phone rang. "No, you stay with Piper and the baby." He listened a little and nodded. "We're in the hall where Cami's office is. Right. If you're sure." Walker turned to his brother. "Jackson heard the information from Piper's office. Don't ask how they know but he's pulling in the parking lot now."

Sawyer nodded as he opened the next office door and walked through the room. As they finished, the inhabitants were instructed to take their belongings and leave, locking their door behind them. As they finished with all the administration offices, they moved to the next wing. Children were quietly being removed from the building by teachers and office staff and still no Camille.

The band teacher rushed up to Sawyer. "I saw Karl walking Camille out of her office. He said she was sick and needed to go home. It didn't dawn on me until much later that we had a notice she wasn't in the office today. I just thought she had tried to come in and found she was too ill."

"Did she say anything?" Sawyer demanded.

"No. She did moan a little, like she wasn't well and I thought she looked very nauseous. I held the door open for them to leave the hall."

"What door and in what direction were they headed?" asked Walker.

The woman pointed in the direction of maintenance. They headed down that corridor.

Chapter 20

Camille was nauseous. She wanted to vomit and knowing that it sometimes made her feel better she tried to see where the bathroom was. Realizing that she was in an unfamiliar place, not her bedroom, she groaned.

"Sorry, sweetheart. I know that you're nauseous. That's why we came down here, away from everyone."

"Karl?" she croaked. Her throat was dry and had a terrible after taste.

"Yes, it's me. I have everything you need until we can go home. It's going to be a long day. Longer than I expected anyway. I didn't want you to be here right now but when you didn't come in, I had to make a new plan." Karl's voice was urgent.

"A new plan? Why? To do what?" She still wanted to puke her guts out but her foggy brain was telling her to pay attention, so she was trying.

"It's Valentine's Day, darling. I have candy, and a steak dinner for you there."

"What? I don't understand. I feel really sick."

"At home. You can make me creamed peas, baked potato, and rolls, all my favorites. I already gave you red roses."

The mention of food made her gagged. "I don't understand." She sat up on what appeared to be an old, discarded sofa.

"I knew you wanted to spend it with me. And after I saw your cheating husband at the Whet Whistle Saturday night, acting like he was single again, well, that was the last straw." His voice turned hard. "I knew you weren't being appreciated or loved. I was willing to wait but now, now we don't have to."

"That was fake. I knew he was there. It was to bring out the person who was harassing me."

"I wasn't harassing. I wanted to warn Sawyer off, but he didn't take the hint." Karl's voice hardened again. "You didn't either."

"Karl," Camille began in what she hoped was a calm, reasonable voice. "I'm pregnant with Sawyer's baby. We are going to be parents again."

"I know and I don't hold you responsible for that. It's obvious that he forced you to submit to him. I would never do that to you."

"I love him, Karl."

"No!" His movements were jerky and his eyes grew wild. "You love me. I've waited for you. I helped you when others were talking about you." He stopped talking and when he next spoke, it was with a calm voice as though he made perfect sense. "I kept telling you that you were mine. I knew you were worried about Sawyer finding out about us too soon. That's why you let him call the police and why you parked in front of the camera. I understood. It was a good move."

Cami didn't know what she should do, so she did nothing. "I don't want to play games. I need some water, please."

Karl hesitated and then pulled his backpack closer. "I made plans for everything." He handed her the water bottle she was almost too weak to open, but he didn't seem to notice. "We will leave here after everyone has gone home. I know the alarm password, you see. And I have the building keys."

She just nodded. Sawyer Knight would never wait that long. And her car was in the lot, up front as it always was these days. You couldn't miss it. She hadn't picked up Lily, so she knew the office would start calling down Lily's long approved pickup list. It would alert more people to there being something wrong. She took a sip of water. It felt good on her throat and she took another sip but stopped. Her stomach wasn't settling very quickly.

"Is there a bathroom here?"

"What? A bathroom?"

"Yes, remember I told you I needed to go more often now that I'm pregnant?"

"The baby, now that is a complication I had to work on but don't worry. I've figured it all out. I couldn't possibly raise someone else's baby." He shook his head as though it was inconceivable. "Besides, I never planned for children. No, not room in my plan for a baby."

"But it's my baby too. If you love me you have to love my baby."

He seemed to think about that for a moment before shaking his head again. "Nope. I never wanted children and you have already had two. I can't share you. Babies take up too much of a person's time. Mother had another baby after me and she spent too much time with him. I kept him from crying. When he stopped moving, mother cried but called someone to take him away. She didn't have him any longer, and she gave me all her attention again. As it should be."

"Where is your mother now?"

"Dead. I wouldn't need another woman if she was still alive. But..." He shrugged as though it were an inconsequential loss. "She's not. Then you came just at the right time to take her place."

"I'm not your mother, Karl."

Her heart was pounding, her overwhelming nausea from the medication he had injected her with had given way to strong reactions based in her fear. Her hands trembled even harder when she felt the baby move. That frightened her. Would he harm her baby like he'd admitted to doing to his baby sibling years ago?

"No, but you can learn how to do things the way she did, and you have had children, you know how to be a mother."

She had to reason with him. Fill the time until her husband could find her. That was if he was even back from the fire. The fire.

"Karl, did you call in the fire today?"

He grinned. "That is what I meant by changing plans. It was a good one, wasn't it? I was especially proud of myself. I knew that meant you would come and pick up Lily. You always did when you were home. I just needed to get you to the building. And that message was genius, wasn't it?"

Sawyer, where are you?

"Karl, I don't recognize this place. Is it near the school?"

His face brightened then became contemplative. He nodded. "It is under the school. Another way I outsmarted people. Those Knight men thought they were so smart. I needed to find a place close enough to wait while the building emptied. A place they couldn't find."

"Sawyer needs help with the children. They are out of school now and he can't watch them and do his work. You know I have a little boy just like your mother had you. He needs me like you needed your mother."

"He has Sawyer. I had only my mom, and she only had me. It was all we needed. It's different if you have someone who can step in, like your boy."

"Sawyer married me and I married him. Don't you think he will look for me?"

"Maybe a little, but it will be just for show. I have already claimed you. I protected you from those women who said nasty things about you. Sawyer knew I'd protect you, that's why he didn't stop me from watching out for you. He stopped calling the police because he accepted the messages. He understood you were mine."

"That was me, Karl. Me. I didn't tell Sawyer about them until this past weekend. We thought it was a woman trying to claim Sawyer. That's why he went to the Whet Whistle Saturday night, to see if he could draw her out."

"No, you're wrong! He knew it was me. He knew. We had an understanding. He even said 'thank you' once. He knew I would be the better man to take care of you or rather you would be the right one to take care of me."

She didn't know what to say. He was living a dream sequence that wasn't based in any reality. Camille worried she'd push him over if she persisted in an area he obviously believed to be true.

But she did need to go to the bathroom. Her bladder was so full it hurt.

"Karl, I really need to go to the bathroom. I'm about to pee my pants."

He seemed to consider that for a moment. "You aren't pulling my leg or anything?"

"No, my side hurts and the pressure in my bladder is painful. If you care about me, you will help me find a bathroom."

"Here, I know where one is. No funny business though."

"No funny business." She got up slowly and walked gingerly to the bathroom. Her relief was in her words. "Thank you. I'll try to be quick."

He took her up some stairs she hadn't noticed before. She recognized this hallway. It held the preschool and kindergarten where her babies went to school. Her heart hurt at the thought she might not see them again but she berated her thinking. She'd get out of here. She and the little one would be safe. They would be home tonight and this nightmare would be over.

How did she miss the signs of Karl doing all these things? Now that she knew, it made as much sense as a woman. She wondered how no one ever caught him and even Sawyer didn't feel like all of this was aimed at her. He, like everyone else, assumed it was a woman. Partly because, after being gone six years, she didn't know many people here, and it started after she arrived in town. She had no idea how Karl got the impression she wanted him or at least wanted to be his surrogate mother. It gave her the creeps.

It sounded like he'd fixated on his mother all those years. How the woman didn't think he needed a therapist for his mental health, she would never know. Likely afraid she would lose him if she told people. Now, he had shifted that fixation to her. Camille wondered how long he had been without his mother. He obviously had a psychologically unhealthy attachment to her as his parent.

"Camille, hurry in and then we need to go back downstairs."

Out came the large key ring, and he opened the bathroom. The toilets were small but at least she'd be able to go to the bathroom. And text! She'd forgotten her phone was in her front pocket, covered by her belly and a big shirt. He stood just inside the bathroom door. She squatted on the tiny toilet and as she peed she texted.

Camille: I am in the kgtn toilets.

Camille: Going back to the basement via the back stairway near Pre-k and K bathrooms.

Camille: Near the couches.

Camille: The MINE person is Karl.

Camille: He's crazy.

Sawyer: We're coming.

She wiped and flushed. Shoving her phone back into her front pocket, she stepped out and washed her hands. Her husband was on his way to save her. Now to just keep Karl calm.

SAWYER TOLD HIS BROTHERS what Camille had texted him. They routed out the police officers and headed for the basement.

"Wait," said Randy Cambridge. "I think I know where the couches are. When I helped with the drama club play set-up last year, there were things in the very back corner of the elementary side of the basement. There is a huge stack of furniture and things. There were couches."

"You know the way?" asked his fellow officer.

"I do." Randy led them to what felt like the bowels of the earth. The school building was old and had been in use for over seventy years. It seemed like that was how many years' worth of debris was inside.

As they approached, they could hear voices that seemed far away. Randy pointed to the furthest, darkest corner and he indicated that they spread out. He pulled Sawyer and his brothers to the side.

"Now listen to me. My guys know how to handle this but you three need to do as I say. Sawyer, your only focus is to grab your wife and get her to safety. Don't worry about anyone or anything else. We will make a distraction and hopefully draw him away. We can handle the rest."

"Got it."

"You two, no heroics," said Randy. "I won't give you any further instructions. That's it. Do what is necessary but not if you are risking your own life. Understood?"

"Yes."

"Yep."

Randy nodded in the direction of the dark corner and they slipped into the shadows.

Camille jerked when they were suddenly surrounded with a loud noise. Almost simultaneously dark figures jumped from out of shadowy thin air. Her arms were grabbed, and she was pulled tightly to a hot, hard chest. She heard an oomph, and furniture was falling all around them. Grunts and crashes were everywhere. She screamed.

"Hush, baby. It's me. It's Sawyer."

Chapter 21

Summer was hot in the hill country. She'd not missed these extreme temperatures when she was in Alaska, but it was a small price to pay for having her family. Pulling into the driveway, Camille was greeted by Sawyer holding back two screeching children. Something must be up. Sawyer sauntered up and opened her door to help her out before opening the back door and scooping their six-week-old from his cool environment. The youngest Knight must have been upset about the change in his comfort level because Colton Sawyer Knight screwed his little face up and squawked.

Colton after his grandfather Knight. Sawyer had wanted his middle name to be Owen, but Cami put her foot down hard on his initials being COK. Finally, Sawyer gave in when she said she wouldn't sign the birth certificate paperwork. He was just vain enough to encourage Sawyer as the substitute of his newest son's middle name.

"You started it by giving Eli my middle name." Yes, she had.

Sawyer had wanted Cami to tender her resignation the very day they discovered Karl was the one who had all but terrorized her for months, but she stuck to her guns and lasted until May when things were too hard. She then offered part-time next year and was quickly accepted. Sawyer was still griping over his losses on that. He'd wanted her to stay home all day.

She was glad that Lily's birthday had passed, and Eli's was next week. Children's parties were exhausting, but she was thankful she could give them one separately this year. It hadn't mattered to either before but evidently Eli had decided boys didn't share birthdays, not with girls anyway.

Her children, their children had grown this last year in so many ways and their parents and grandparents had as well. When her father had learned of Cami's pregnancy, he began coming out to the ranch to mend relationships. Cami's mother had come twice since Colton's birth. It was a start.

"How's Mama and little man?"

"Both perfect."

"I knew that."

He kissed her slowly, something he had been doing lately. She had made sure they stuck to their guns and waited for the six-week postpartum checkup before he could be with her again. Doc had recommended abstaining the last month because she was so tired and Sawyer had been on board with that. Then he found out there were a minimum of six weeks he had to wait for being with his wife again after the birth and Sawyer Knight was getting a little testy. Lately, he was acting as though he were near death over it.

He leaned into her to whisper in her ear, "I meant are we good to have sex?"

She smiled up at him because she was feeling the strain as well. "Yep. You're all clear for take-off."

"Now that's what I wanted to hear, darlin'. Tonight's the night." She shook her head and grinned. He was predictable.

Eli and Lily had waited long enough and came barreling to their mother. "Mama, we have a surprise for you." Eli was bursting with excitement.

"You do?"

"Yes. Come see," Lily said her piece and was racing to the barn.

She looked up at Sawyer who was holding their little bundle of boy in his carrier. "What is it, a litter of kittens?"

"It's definitely new but I'm not spoiling their surprise."

"Sawyer, it's too hot to stay out here for long. It must be ninety-five degrees."

"Ninety-seven, now get moving."

As they entered the barn nearest the house, the kids were standing next to a beautiful Buckskin. "Mama, Daddy got this for you! Isn't he beautiful?"

"He is beautiful." She turned to Sawyer. "He really is handsome."

"I went to an auction last week and saw him. After I got him home and worked with him, I knew he'd be perfect for you. Gentle, well-trained, but with spunk."

"Like me?" she grinned.

"I wish. Two out of three isn't bad though." She punched his arm and he faked injury. "Reminds me. Now that you're healed, it's time to pay for all those naughty moments during the last nine months."

"See that bundle of joy you're holding? Remember those five hours of labor I was in? Yeah, I paid my dues, believe me."

"You sure did. Here's Colt. Go inside and take the kids. It's hot and I still have some work to do." He dropped another kiss on her lips. "Not everyone is wimpy."

LITTLE COLTON WAS A good sleeper and kept to a schedule almost religiously. Like his daddy, thought Camille. She had taken a shower first so she could nurse before her little man fell asleep. They still had him in their room because she could feed at night better that way. She'd gotten a nap with Lily and the baby, so she wasn't as tired as she often was this time of night.

Sawyer walked out of the shower, naked as the day he was born. He strutted into the bedroom, never a man to have any qualms about his body or displaying it for her visual enjoyment. And enjoy, she did. He was a handsome man, his body honed by hard work, and he was gentle as a lamb with his children.

He lifted the bassinet that Colton was sleeping in and placed it in the small little room off the bedroom. Cami liked him close, but she didn't complain when Sawyer moved him. Tonight, was their night. The night they had been waiting for since she had gotten too uncomfortable to have sex. It was on nights like these that she was glad the doors were solid wood.

"Strip, baby. Daddy has some things he wants to do tonight, and clothes are not required."

"You sure we won't wake up the baby?"

"I'm sure he won't remember what we were doing if we do."

She laughed. "True."

She took her nightshirt off in record time; suddenly remembering her baby belly was still anchored like a flabby albatross around her waist. "Maybe I'll just slide under the covers."

"Nope. You stop those thoughts right now. You are the woman who carried my children in her belly so carefully and then gave birth to them. That's unselfish love and you aren't hiding the evidence of that love from me."

"I'll do some exercises and it will go away. Well, most of it."

"Okay, if that's what you want but don't do it for me. I don't care. You, however much of you there is, belongs to me."

"So, I've heard, 'Keep the belly, it looks good on you. I'm no longer into toned tummies.' Got it."

He swatted her butt leaving a sting that brought on a familiar tingle she hadn't experienced in quite this way since he last paddled her in foreplay nearly a year ago.

"Brat. Now, the changes in these lovely ladies, I do care about. I think I should check them out, don't you?"

"Carefully. I'm still tender."

He gently took one nipple into his mouth and curled his tongue, lapping up the droplets of milk that escaped from them. "No wonder he loves nursing. This is the best dessert ever."

She giggled. He sucked lightly, then more intensely as his girl begged him to continue. She'd longed for this intimacy since discovering her pregnancy. They'd made love more times than she could count but the anticipation tonight stole her breath, leaving her gulping in air when her body demanded it.

"Sawyer," she moaned. "Daddy, spank me?"

"Are you asking me to smack your bottom, little girl?"

Her lady's bits zinged with arousal. "Yes."

"Daddy."

She hesitated, lifting her eyes to his full of demanding expectation. She needed this man. "Daddy," she said coyly. "Please, Daddy?"

She drew her breath in sharply as his hands kneaded her breasts, rubbing the drops of milk around the nipples. It felt so good she thought she'd be lost in the sensation before she ever climaxed. His tenderness was interspersed with brusque tweaks that drew agonized moans from her lips.

His cock was pushing against her wet crease, teasing, taunting her cravings to new heights. He reached down between them after releasing her now leaking, aching nipples to introduce his finger along the seam of her core. Her clit was hard and stiff when he tapped it. A butterfly flutter and he was gone, but it was enough to encourage her to push her hips up in response, as if on a marionette's strings.

He slapped her pussy. It stung. She grunted her disapproval and swatted his arm when she saw the satisfaction on his face.

"Mean."

"Did you just smack your daddy, little girl?"

"Yes. You slapped my pussy."

"Hmm, you mean this?" He did it again. She cried out, arching into the hand he left in place. "You put yourself and our baby at risk by keeping secrets, Cami. And you tried to handle that crazy Karl alone."

She moaned. "I didn't know it was him."

"You didn't know who it was so you should have let me handle it."

She wiggled her discomfort at his words. He slapped her pussy again. She hissed.

"Yes, Daddy," she pouted.

"Still stubborn. It's good sometimes. I like it, but when your safety is at stake, I will never allow it. Roll over. This daddy wants to spank his naughty girl and then he's going to take her thoroughly."

She rolled over slowly, feeling his hand slide across her hips, caressing her lower cheeks as she wiggled into place. He massaged harder, heating her skin with the rougher touches.

"Yesss..." A stinging hand landed on her gyrating ass. She hissed. Time to give over to him, let him take her where he would, using the path he chose. He always brought her to paradise in the end.

"Be still and take your punishment like a good girl."

Sawyer savored the heat from her bottom and in his hand. He loved touching her and spanking her was the ultimate touch. He heard her distressed "Uh," and it brought an immediate smile to his face. His Cami had a love hate relationship with spanking. It got him off just thinking of her joyful angst. How his cock could stiffen even further he had no idea.

He leaned down to whisper in her ear. "Up on your knees and face on the bed. You know how I want you."

He handled his dick as she slowly slid into place. He released himself to slap her inner thigh. "Spread them wide, naughty girl. You know how I like you. This is defiance and I will have to address that."

His whole body tingled as he watched the honey drip from her pussy. She tried to suppress a shiver; he watched her tense as she succumbed to his lovemaking. He slapped her bottom in earnest now, keeping the rhythm and severity below her tolerance level but intense to keep her torment at the arousal stage.

He dipped his finger into her honey well and drew it up several times to her back entrance, slapping her inner thighs three times each with a bite when she didn't immediately return to the position he had demanded. Crying out, he introduced his index finger as she was preoccupied with her response.

Slowly moving in and out of her darkest place, he said quietly with considerable sternness, "Put your ass in the air, young lady, and do not move. Not one inch while I play."

She dipped her bottom one last time as he landed three more hard slaps to it. She gushed and he brought more of her essence to her backside. She stayed in place as he introduced two fingers inside her, then three. In, spread, out, again. Soon she was bucking and whining at the intrusion and the removal both.

He loved her neediness and touched her clit lightly, felt her muscles tightened around his fingers as she came. Her dripping pussy coated his hand as he coaxed her orgasm on, extending it to lengths he hadn't seen her go before. He removed his fingers and kissed her ass, licking her dripping arousal as he speared her sex with his tongue.

He positioned himself behind her and glided into her dripping sheath with a sigh. There were still little muscle tremors from her orgasm. He could feel her exposed clit, stiff and vulnerable. Taking her slowly at first, not wanting to hurt his girl in any way, although it was difficult to restrain himself after such a long dry spell. He wanted her so much.

The love he had for Cami had grown to a level he never would have believed. He had thought he loved her completely before she left town, but this last year had taught him so much. She was more than he had ever imagined all those years ago when he found her riding that pony with her friends.

She had taken all of what was good between them away when she'd left without warning. Then suddenly she'd returned, bringing him more than he had ever dreamed. The happiness he had now was more than he had a right to, but he'd not let a moment of it pass without appreciating her gifts to him. He would spend the rest of his life giving her all he had to give in exchange for what she gave him.

"Mmm. So good, Daddy. I'm sleepy now."

"Sleep baby. I've got you."

Lying next to his girl, his woman, who nourished them all with her love, he drew her sweaty body to his, curled his strength around her protectively, and sighed in complete contentment as he heard her little snore of relaxed sleep. He did that for her. Protected her, cared for her, loved her. And he always would.

The End

About the Author
Alyssa Bailey

USA Today Bestselling Author of Sassy Romance that is realistic and sensual with a touch of suspense. A dyed in the wool Texan living in Alaska for half her life, Alyssa now divides her time between the beauty of Southeast Alaska and the piney woods of East Texas. She enjoys taking from her own experiences to create series in fictitious worlds sure to tease the reader's palate and invite them to sink into exciting adventures.

Alyssa enjoys writing consensual power exchanges between intelligent, sassy women who are not afraid to make a stand and loving men confident enough to give his woman space but masterful enough to keep her indulged and protected. There is *always* a happily ever after.

Visit me online and sign up for my Newsletter:
http://alyssabailey.com[1]
Join my Facebook Page for fun and prizes:
https://www.facebook.com/alyssabailey.romance

Other Books By Alyssa Bailey

Safe and Secure Series: Contemporary, suspense, spicy
    Saving Sharlee
Saving Jessie
Saving Ivy
Saving Mallory
Saving Callie
Saving Becky
Saving Oakley
Saving Finley (2023)

CLEARWATER DADDIES Trilogy -Contemporary, Spicy
    Piper's Plan
Camille's Second Chance
Josie's Refuge

DARLING DUCHESSES: Regency, Daddy Dom, Spicy
    The Devil Duke's Little Distraction
The Daring Duke's Little Impulse

GUARDIANS OF REFUGE (Contemporary, Military, Spicy)

SEAL of Refuge
The Strategy of Love
The Tactics of Love
The Mandate of Love

Sage County (Cowboy, Contemporary, Spicy)
Deep Waters
Still Waters

IN THE SPIRIT OF CHRISTMAS -Contemporary, Sweet
Christmas Wishes and You

ANTHOLOGIES (HEAT VARIES)
Sweet Town Love
Historical Heroes
Hero to Obey (limited time)
Cowboy for a Cause (limited time)
Naughty 12 Days of Christmas 2017

MULTI-AUTHOR BOX SETS (Heat Level Various)
Love, Christmas 2 Recipes
Irresistible Heroes
Sweet and Sassy Summertime Vol. 2
Dear Santa: A Christmas Wish
Sweet and Sassy New Beginnings

Audiobooks
Accepting His Ways
Her Sweet Complication
His Gentle Persuasion
Quinlan's Quest
Lady Caroline's Defiance

Don't miss out!

Visit the website below and you can sign up to receive emails whenever Alyssa Bailey publishes a new book. There's no charge and no obligation.

https://books2read.com/r/B-A-MXIL-VWVMC

BOOKS 2 READ

Connecting independent readers to independent writers.

Did you love *Camille's Second Chance*? Then you should read *Piper's Plan* by Alyssa Bailey!

Piper has plans, but they defy Daddy's rules. Things could get hot.

Piper Gentry was not one to back down from a challenge, not in her international investments company or in her personal life. Piper looks for sense in her father's death while looking for ways to make the family ranch profitable again in the wild heat of a Texas summer.

Jackson Knight has always loved Piper Gentry. Being her husband and Daddy, raising their family on the ranch is all he has ever wanted, but she never returned from college. Now she's back and his challenge is to remind her that his plans are still her plans and that she feels the same about him. He'll stop at nothing to keep her near him and safe.

Piper's plans do not involve taking orders from anyone, including Jackson, but her longing for what they once had, has her doubting herself. Who will pose the greatest threat to her safety—outsiders eager to get their hands on her family legacy, or Piper herself?

Read more at alyssabailey.com.

Also by Alyssa Bailey

Clearwater Daddies
Camille's Second Chance

Watch for more at alyssabailey.com.